Something Familiar

By S.N.Arly

Copyright

Something Familiar

First Printing: 2019

ISBN: 978-0-9913209-4-3
Library of Congress Control Number: 2019905975

The Write Mann, LLC
St. Paul, MN 55106
www.TheWriteMann.com

Cover design by Shareen Mann and Beren Fox.
Cover photos by Adrian Bar and AK¥N Cakiner, provided by Unsplash.

Author photo by Ben Huset, Diversicon 2018.

Library of Congress Cataloging-in-Publication Data

Names: S.N.Arly, author
Title: Something Familiar / S.N.Arly
Description: Trade Paperback First Edition | St. Paul | The Write Mann, 2019
Identifiers: LCCN 2019905975 | ISBN: 978-0-9913209-4-3(trade pbk | 978-0-9913209-5-0 (electronic/epub)
LC record available at https://lccn.loc.gov/2019905975

Acknowledgements

The act of writing is generally a solo affair, but when you have a family, it becomes a bit more of a production out of necessity. My greatest appreciation goes to my husband Steve for helping protect my writing time, even when I don't seem to have a specific project going on. I am also grateful to my children Beren and Ranna, who listened to the rough drafts with great enthusiasm; I hope I can be as supportive of your interests as you are of mine.

I have relied on the encouragement and constructive feedback from other writers to improve and grow. To the members of Guts and Rocks, Katie Ferreira & Dana Baird, I greatly appreciate the time you took to give me honest and useful feedback on this. Without you, the 'creepy, eew' factor might still be present. Thanks, also, to Eric Heideman, who invited me to read the first few chapters of this at DreamHaven Books in March 2019.

My friends and followers on my website, Tumblr and AO3 have been a fantastic source of motivation when days were long and enthusiasm was low. So thanks also to: aknazer, BBWoulfC, beany846, bowser14456, h-sunnywet-d, EnberLight, Hilzabub, Lairep, LazyWorkaholic, LNC, mardimari, Momontra, peachgreentea, perditalottachocolate, seasonofthegeek, tbehartoo, Tjikicew, youcancallmecirce, and Zelphaba.

Table of Contents

Chapter One

"I know you're there." The man's voice was as harsh and cold as Jacque remembered, and a jolt of fear shot through his chest, freezing him as surely as a binding spell. "You may as well come out now. You can't defy me or my magic, and if you cooperate, I may feel gracious when assigning your punishment."

Jacque had been hopeful at first. While his father had alerted the police and media of his son's disappearance, he'd left out a fairly significant detail regarding Jacque's nature. And now the man was walking the neighborhood streets of the fourteenth arrondissement alone in the dark. He still didn't want anyone to find out; he thought he could bide his time and use others' magic to bring Jacque to heel. He knew nothing of cats.

For the last four months, Jacque had lived as a stray cat on the streets of Paris. It may not have been the easiest life, but it was a thousand times better than living with his all too human father. He would rather die than go back to being a prisoner in that house, denied the opportunity to be what he really was.

He wasn't sure how his father had found him; Pierre

Parenteau was a gifted designer but a mediocre magic user. He relied on other people's spells and enchantments to get his way. But he was successful and wealthy, and he'd probably purchased a locating talisman this time. Jacque suspected there were ways to inhibit such tools from finding him, but he had no way of learning this for himself. His magic education involved being on the receiving end of his father's personal or bought enchantments and charms.

Jacque closed his brilliant green eyes and tapped into his feline nature. Leaning on his human logic and education had helped him get by quite well, really, but thinking like a sixteen-year old runaway boy was not going to get him out of this.

Settling all four paws on the moss-covered cobblestone sidewalk, he peered out from behind the large planter. As a black cat, the night was his time. As a committed stray, the back streets and rooftops were his place. His father would not catch him here. He embraced his instinct, tempered it with logic, and simply **felt** when the opportune moment hit. He darted out, bounding down the street to a thickly vine-covered trellis.

"Stop!" his father ordered.

Jacque scaled the vines, scampering across them where they spanned the width of the street. He growled as he passed directly over his father to a nearby roof. Twice, he felt a very faint tug, as if his father was reaching for the old bonds Jacque spent every day eroding. His own magic was minimal, most of it related to shape-shifting, but his time on the street had shown him that if he worked at it, he had the ability to curse things with misfortune. The triggers for his father's compulsion spells were his first experiments; they were in tatters at this point, barely present enough to notice.

He reached the roof just in time for his father to throw a compact spell at him. His aim was worse than his magic, and it missed. Jacque hissed at the explosion of gold sparks, spitting out the cat equivalent of, "fuck you." He kept his distance from the

2

newly conjured cage. On the off chance that his father had purchased more of those, and that his first shot was merely unlucky, Jacque scrambled away from the edge of the roof, so he wouldn't be vulnerable to ground attacks.

This was the second time his father had found him, and he'd clearly stepped up his game. Jacque was going to need to rethink his situation to prevent a third opportunity.

Chapter Two

Brigitte sat on the low curb between the cobbled street and sidewalk. Her black braids hung over her shoulders to dangle between her knees as she stared at the moss under her feet. She didn't want to admit it to anyone, but she was beginning to feel more than a little disappointed. She'd waited much longer than any of her witch-born friends to find her familiar. Most got their familiars at fourteen, and her cousins in China had theirs by thirteen. Yet here she was, sixteen and completely devoid of a familiar. It was getting a little embarrassing, but she'd wanted to be sure she was ready for the commitment of a permanent bond. Everything she'd read suggested this would ultimately give her and her familiar a stronger and more satisfying connection. But finding her cat wasn't going well at all.

Instead of picking a random purebred or pet store kitten, her magic wanted her to select a stray, and that there needed to be a connection when they met. Maybe she was being too difficult. She'd started her search on the streets near her parents' *boulangerie pâtisserie* and potion shop in the thirteenth arrondissement with no luck. Master Fu, who was both a regular customer at the shop and

4

a good friend of her maman's, suggested she look near his acupuncture parlor. He'd been visited several times by a black cat that he thought would be a good fit. He insisted the tom was young enough to be flexible and he didn't belong to anyone despite his sweet temperament. He'd also said something about matching chi and other conditions considered favorable by Chinese witch-born. She'd searched the entire Chinese Quarter without spotting a free cat, much less any who were black. Either Master Fu's tom had moved on, or he'd been picked up already. The witch population of Paris was not small, and it was public knowledge that cats without an obvious claim, were considered fair game.

She'd moved to the nearby fourteenth arrondissement in the hope that there would be a suitable stray lurking in the street-side container gardens, the boulevard trees, or the clumps of vines climbing up the walls and draping across the narrow streets. To be fair, she had found several cats of varying ages, but none had be the right one. Her magic's reaction was lackluster to all of them, and none seemed to ask her to take them home.

A couple of her friends suggested she just pick one and be done with it, but that wasn't Brigitte's way. She'd put it off this long, and it was worth waiting. She was going to find the right cat, no matter how long it took. She took a deep breath, reaching out with her magic, surprised to find several cats nearby. Perhaps today wasn't as hopeless as it had seemed.

* * *

Jacque sniffed at the air. **She** was back. It was enough to rouse him from his rooftop spot in the waning evening sun so he could observe her again. His paws were light, pattering against the concrete ledge jutting out from the second story windows of the apartment building he'd been using as a central point for his activity this week. From here, he could nestle in behind lush vines and watch the street below without being spotted, though it would only be a few more weeks before these vines were bare. Feeling her reach out with her magic, he closed his eyes and basked in the warmth for a moment. His father's magic had **never** felt like this, not even in the days before the bindings and the cuffs. The difference made him curious, but his memories of painful magic were still too fresh.

Her long black hair swung and dangled in braids that seemed to taunt him. He had no doubt they would be fun to pounce at and tug, at least until she caught hold of him. She had Asian features, but pale freckled skin. She looked about his age, which seemed a bit odd. He'd always heard witches tended to get their familiars much younger. Had she been unable to form a bond with an animal until now? Given her unaided strength, that seemed unlikely. He just didn't know enough.

"Hello lovelies," she said, putting down a little cup of milk for the two strays who'd already approached her. Moving slowly, she reached into a pocket and pulled out another container. When she opened it, the aroma of chicken filled the air.

He really missed chicken, but it wasn't enough to draw him in. She was a witch, and he'd always been warned that witches could not be trusted. The meat was enough to summon Miss Gigi, a bonded familiar who lived in the area. He'd met the blue-eyed Birman cat briefly in passing, but he'd been reluctant to trust her. For her part, she clearly found him peculiar. Experience with his father's familiar told him that elevated cats were just as dangerous as their magic users.

"Good evening, madame," the girl said brightly. She offered Miss Gigi a bit of the meat, but made no move to touch her. "I can see you're not for me, but you deserve a treat, too."

Though skittish, the two strays wriggled and pounced in their enthusiasm for fresh meat, a rare find on the streets of Paris. When

Jacque expected the girl to scoop one of them up, she simply reached out to scratch under their chins. Wasn't she supposed to be stealing them away? If she couldn't afford a purebred or shelter cat, shouldn't she be desperate? That definitely wasn't the vibe she gave off.

He felt eyes on him, and looked down to Miss Gigi who had finished her treat and was watching where he sat in the shadows. When he met her eyes, she glanced at the witch and then back at him. She wasn't calling him out, but she was definitely trying to get a message across.

Once the milk and meat were gone, the girl gave out a few more pets before packing away her thermos. "Thank you for visiting with me," she said, a happy smile on her face. "I'm afraid that none of you are for me." She bowed to Miss Gigi. "Merry meet, madame." She nodded to the other two strays. "If you are to end up as familiars, I hope you find good matches." Dusting off her hands, she slowly stood up.

When the girl was gone, Miss Gigi turned to him. "You should keep an eye on that one," she meowed at him. "She might be just what you need."

* * *

Brigitte clenched her teeth a bit as she started on her way home. She'd have homework to keep her occupied, but it was so hard not to despair. Papa had been adamant that she take all the time she needed to find the right fit, releasing Brigitte from her usual after-school shift at the shop. Maman had urged her to cherish this time in her life, because once she bonded with a familiar, a whole new stage of life would open to her.

Sniffling, she rubbed briskly at her eyes before any tears could fall. Today's kittens had been sweet, and she wouldn't have gotten to meet them if she'd already found her cat. While she couldn't fully speak with the familiar who'd come out to see her, she'd gotten the distinct impression that she wanted Brigitte to come back tomorrow. She had some plans to help her, and really, that was very kind. The pretty Birman's actions actually made her feel much better, now that she thought about it. She owed Brigitte nothing, yet she offered to help. Witches didn't often get to work with others' familiars, so this was a rare opportunity, a gift. She could be content with that.

Chapter Three

He couldn't get the witch girl out of his head. He'd seen her the last three days, and each time it was the same. She wandered the alleys until she found a cat or two to… well… visit. There was no catnip to lure them, something he'd seen with other witch-born. The milk and morsels weren't tainted, so she wasn't killing off strays or binding them into some sort of army. It was all quite cordial. She never chased anyone, choosing to let them come to her. He'd seen a particularly skittish kitten lurk three meters away while her litter-mates scarfed rewards, and instead of compelling the stray, the girl used her magic to deliver a few pieces of meat so the little one wouldn't miss out on a free meal.

He didn't question why he was able to find her again. He was a black cat, for the moment at least, and he was more than a little sensitive to magic, which had actually made living with his father all the more painful. He did wonder why he was bothering to stalk her. She was looking for a familiar, and she'd made that clear, but he couldn't begin to guess what would make a cat or kitten the right one. So far, none of the strays had met her requirements, and with his brand of magic he didn't stand a chance.

He shook his head, hesitating before continuing on his path in search of the sweet witch. He didn't want to be a familiar. He'd run away from home to escape the bindings his father imposed on him. Why on Gaia, would he seek out permanent magical entanglements? Of course he didn't want to be a familiar. He was a stray, and that's how he'd live until he turned eighteen, or maybe the rest of his life. It was better this way.

He'd dreamed of her, though. Every night since he first saw her, he'd woken to an almost painful absence of safety and warmth. It didn't make sense. He didn't know her, and while she seemed so kind, it could still all be a ruse. He needed to monitor her. That would keep his worries over the insidious creeping thoughts and cozy dreams at bay.

He continued on his way, again hiding himself in the shadows and leaves to watch her. Her clothes were bright and fun, reflecting a spirited personality. Other than her jacket, she'd had a different outfit each time, and they were all equally fabulous. For all his years modeling clothes by countless designers, he'd never been permitted to express himself like that. He doubted even his father could object to her impeccable styling. Today she wore a white swing tunic top with cherry blossom embroidery peeking out of her open coat. He suspected her pink pants were denim, but couldn't tell from here. His cat eyes saw color better than regular cats, but not as well as his human eyes did. He hadn't seen pastel denim since the Italian women's fashion week three years ago.

Miss Gigi proudly strolled into the alley, a short line of strays following behind her. When the girl bent down with her cup of milk, Miss Gigi nudged the free cats to approach. Jacque grinned, flicking his tongue against his delightfully sharp teeth. She was trying to help the girl, like some sort of familiar matchmaker. It was adorable.

This time things went a little differently, and he held his breath as the girl scooped up a gray tabby from the little clowder.

Had she found her familiar? Why did that make his chest hurt?

"Oh dear," she said softly. "You have ear mites." She fondled the cat's ears, and looked up to meet Miss Gigi's eyes. "I'd like to treat his ears. Can you let him know I'm not going to harm him?"

Miss Gigi bobbed her head and let out a series of meows and mrrows. "Sit still and let the witchling cure your ears. You'll be grateful for it later."

The cat sat docile while the girl dripped a minty smelling potion on his ears and waved a hand over his head. Jacque felt the magic, even from his hiding place. Again, it was nothing like his father's, leaving him soothed, instead of anxious.

"There you go," the girl said. "Good as new." She gently set the cat back down and finished doling out treats. "Thank you for coming to see me," she told the cats. "And I do appreciate your help, madame." She bowed to Miss Gigi. "I'm afraid I've got to go." She cleaned up her things, reaching to give Miss Gigi a bit of meat before heading out.

Miss Gigi sat where she was, long after the girl had left. She looked up to the shadows. "Did you think she was going to pick that little tom?" she meowed. "How did that feel?"

He took a three-hop route down to the alley beside her. "She wouldn't want me," he insisted, choosing not to answer her questions. He still wasn't sure how he felt about the inexplicable moment of fear and sorrow.

"She's powerful, and you're sensitive," Miss Gigi continued. "You're exactly what she wants."

"Not... exactly," he replied. He wasn't fully cat, and he was pretty sure Miss Gigi knew that.

"**You** aren't meant to be a stray," she hissed. "You're clever and resourceful, I've no doubt you'll handle the winter fine, but this is the wrong life for you." She stared into his eyes for a moment before turning away. "There is an opportunity before you."

"An opportunity to be enslaved?" he asked.

Miss Gigi laughed. "That girl will not be enslaving her familiar. She's looking for a partner, a companion. Why do you think it's taking so long?"

Jacque was quiet for a moment. Miss Gigi was contradicting everything his father claimed witches would do if they found him.

"Do you want respect and affection?" Miss Gigi asked. "For those will be your fate, should you go with that girl."

He stared at his paws a moment. "How can you be sure? People change." His father had never been exactly warm to him, but when his mother was still around, he'd seemed fond enough of Jacque. That all changed when she vanished.

"My witch is gifted in reading the currents of time and chance," Miss Gigi said. "As her familiar, I'm a fair paw at seeing." She got to her feet. "Think hard on this, child, and don't let it pass by without making an actual decision on it." She turned and trotted away, her tail twisting behind her.

* * *

He led the witch on a quick and merry jaunt to this alley. It was quiet and empty, and had decent hiding places, allowing him to control their meeting. As he'd hoped, she started following him the moment she caught sight of him. He was careful to go slow and stop periodically so she could track him, without turning it into a chase, since she'd made it clear she wouldn't run at the cats she met.

"Here, kitty kitty," she called, her voice light and playful.

He liked her voice, even though it had haunted his dreams since the first time he heard it.

She closed her eyes, and he felt her magic lightly brush over him. Smiling happily, she crouched down and pulled out the thermos he'd seen so often. "Come on, kitty. I just want to meet you." There was no lie in her words, and she looked content to wait.

* * *

Brigitte relaxed, prepared to sit for some time if that would draw him out, but it wasn't necessary. He was hungry or curious, and brave enough to approach. She opened her eyes when she sensed him half a meter away. He was sleek and perfectly black, with hair somewhere between medium and long, and it lay smooth and clean over his whole body. His eyes, oh goodness, his eyes were such a beautiful green.

"Oh," she gasped. "You're gorgeous, aren't you?"

He paused and rolled his shoulder to gaze at her over it, before slowly taking a few more steps.

Giggling at his posing, she pushed the thermos cap of milk toward him, then pulled her hands back, keen to get to know him without spooking him. "I suppose you know what a handsome lad you are, huh?" He was out of his kitten days, but he had the leggy build of an adolescent. "Do all the ladies admire you?"

* * *

"Mrrrrow," he agreed, pausing to smell the milk. Then he leaned forward just a bit to sniff at her. Her skin was warm against his nose, and he butted his forehead against her fingers. His magic sense kicked into overdrive at her touch. When she ran her hand over his head and back, he suddenly remembered the joy in being petted. His mother had given him all sorts of pats and cuddles no matter his form, and he wondered how he'd survived without it for so long.

"Oh, goodness, you're so soft." She scratched his neck, hitting all the best places, though she seemed to be verifying his lack of collar. "Don't you know how dangerous it is to prowl the streets with no tag or necklace, *Hēi Māo?*" she asked.

Had she just named him? And in Mandarin, one of the

13

languages his father insisted he study? It may have been intended as a nickname or term of endearment, since it was literally a description of what he was, but he was suddenly determined get rid of his old name and use the one she'd given him instead. He rubbed his head against her forearm, lifting his front paws to her knee in an effort to raise his jaw enough to reach her face. If he became her familiar, he would never be alone again. He wouldn't have to worry about hiding from his father, or other witches for that matter, and he'd be guaranteed a place where he belonged. If he was safe, and she got the benefit of a familiar, it was a fair trade. It was like Miss Gigi had said, they were a good fit for each other; he felt that now, though he suspected that might be the magic.

She ran a hand over his back and drew on her power as she looked him over. Again, he found himself relaxing under her touch.

"Huh." She put a second hand on him. "You have the strangest aura. It's almost as if you're not quite a cat, but at the same time, you really are."

She wasn't wrong, of course. His witch was so clever, and yes, she was his; he could feel it. His purr rumbled up in a way it hadn't in years.

"Are you Schrödinger's cat, then? Both cat yet not cat at the same time?" she asked, smiling brightly.

He purred, amused with her quantum physics joke.

She let out a sigh. "I don't think I can claim you, Hēi Māo, but I'd really like to."

His witch was silly. He'd already decided. He was hers. Her fingers moved under his chin, and he closed his eyes in pleasure.

Chapter Four

His tiny kitty motor encouraged her to keep petting him. Her magic reacted to him as it hadn't for any other cat, urging her to sweep him up and take him home, but her logical brain advised caution.

She let out a sigh, utterly stumped. She didn't feel right claiming him without making sure he was truly available and willing to lock himself into a life-long contract. It was her excessive caution that resulted in her being the only unpaired sixteen-year-old witch at her entire *lycée*. Any claim of ownership that had been on him was shredded, something he would have had to do himself, so clearly he'd left home of his own volition. From everything she'd read, he was legally and magically available. Maybe her parents could help confirm that... though this was supposed to be her decision.

He was more interested in attention than food, which made her worry about how he'd been treated. If she left him out here, someone less scrupulous would snatch him, she was sure of it. "I don't think I can leave you here. It's just not safe for a sweetie like you."

He crawled fully into her lap.

15

"Ooh," she sighed, a little breathless. "I'll bring you home with me, then. And… I guess if you decide you like me, you can be my familiar, and I can be your witch. Does that sound okay?"

His response was to burrow close to her belly, purring louder.

She dipped her finger in the milk and offered it to him. His scratchy little tongue made quick work, his sharp teeth grazing her skin, but not biting.

She recapped the thermos, tucking it back into her bag, then stood, cradling Hēi Māo in her arms. "Do you want to stay in my jacket?" she asked.

He pressed his whole body against her in response. She was pretty sure that was right up there with his aura for odd. Usually it took a while, and a ritual of contract before familiars and witches understood each other at all, and it took even more time before they were good at it.

"Okay, then." She tightened the belt on her jacket to keep Hēi Māo from sliding out the bottom once she stood up, and buttoned the next two buttons. He moved around a little, careful not to scratch, then settled in where he could lean against her while peeking out of the front of her coat. "I promise, I'm going to take good care of you."

He let out a small, "mow," of agreement, as though he had similar plans. But that was definitely wishful thinking.

Dusk was settling over the city as Brigitte approached her family's *boulangerie pâtisserie* and potion shop. With the shadows lengthening, she was glad of the added warmth of Hēi Māo's body tucked into her coat. "We're almost home," she told him. "Just at the end of this block." His little head peeked out of her coat again, and his purr picked up. "If you like it, it can be your home, too. Yeah?" She curled her finger under his chin, and he rubbed against it. "Yeah," she whispered.

The bell jingled overhead as she pulled the door open. The

black cat looked up at it, then around the room, curious, but not spooked.

"Good boy," she murmured.

Her maman was behind the counter, boxing up bread and pastries to drop off at the women's shelter once they closed. "Oh, Brigitte. I was wondering when you'd–" She broke off and stared at the front of her daughter's coat. "Nik," she called, her voice going hoarse. "Come see what your daughter dragged in."

"One moment, Ling," her papa called from deep within the kitchen. "Oh, is it what we hoped for?" There was a scuffle and clank as he finished whatever he was doing.

Without looking away, Maman set aside the pastries and rounded the counter to slowly approach, her hands alternating between out and open, and clutching at her cheeks. "Oh, sweetie, his eyes... he's lovely." She didn't reach forward, though it was obvious she wanted to. It was incredibly rude to touch another witch's familiar without express permission, and even then it was discouraged. "Is he all black?"

Brigitte nodded, catching sight of the tears in her mother's eyes. Maman had lost her familiar in an attack at the Trocadéro when Brigitte was just a baby. She'd been too heartbroken to even consider a replacement. In time, Papa's familiar bound herself to both her parents; it was a little unusual, but not completely unheard of.

"Oh ho!" her papa said happily, stepping out of the kitchen. He was a giant of a Frenchman, and while Brigitte inherited just enough of his height that she might make average stature, her strong Chinese features and lighter build favored her maman. "Success this time?" He wrapped an arm around his tiny wife. "He seems so calm, Brigitte. Did you use a catnip lure?"

Brigitte vehemently shook her head. "I didn't bring any. I didn't want to resort to that."

Her papa chuckled. "What's his name."

Brigitte bit her lip. "Umm. I'm calling him Hēi Māo for now, because I'm not sure if he wants to keep me. It feels wrong to name him… at least until I know." She stroked his head lightly. "He ran away from his last home." He rolled in the nest of her jacket to look up at her, batting gently at her chin, his claws safely tucked in.

"Oooh," her maman half-squealed. "He definitely likes you."

"His aura seems odd to me," Brigitte pointed out. "Like he's cat but not cat at the same time."

Her maman scrutinized Hēi Māo for a moment. "Oh. I see what you mean."

"It made me worry that he's not really meant to be a familiar," Brigitte added. "I'd hate to lock him into something that might be a bad fit for him."

"His chi is compatible with yours," her maman said. "It's a **very** favorable match." She shook her head. "And it's probably what drew him to you."

"Really?" Brigitte hadn't been blessed with the ability to see chi, and she wondered if Hēi Māo was the tom Master Fu had mentioned weeks ago.

"Black cats carry a fair bit of their own magic," her maman said, reaching over to pat Brigitte's shoulder, but drawing back before she could accidentally touch Hēi Māo. "It'll amplify yours, but there are usually a few quirks along the way. That's probably all there is to it."

Brigitte scooped her maybe-familiar out of her jacket, cradling him in both arms. "I guess I remember hearing that somewhere."

Her papa grinned. "Because they have their own magic, they generally get to pick their witch, rather than the other way 'round."

"Really?"

Papa nodded. "They can resist our summons even if they aren't bound to one of us, unlike most cats. And they're immune to a lot of the simpler tricks to catch a cat." He shrugged. "They can still be caught by force, of course, but it takes some doing. I think that little guy knows full well what he's in for, and he picked you."

Brigitte pressed her face gently against Hēi Māo's side. "Aren't you a clever kitty," she whispered.

A much louder purr rumbled out of him.

"See," her papa said with a smile. "He agrees."

Chapter Five

Hēi Māo looked around his witch's room, surprised how comfortable he felt here. The walk up to the family's apartment above the shop felt oddly like coming home. It was bright and open, welcoming. Her room with its light pink walls and high-lofted bed in the corner had a similar feel. She had some sort of craft space under the bed, with a wall-mounted desk extending in both directions from the corner. A sewing machine sat on one end, with tidy folded pieces of fabric beside it. She had a computer and some textbooks on the other section of the desk.

"Until we can screen you for illness, or go through the purification of a binding, you're going to need to stay up in my room," she explained, as if he could understand. A regular cat wouldn't, of course, and he wasn't sure how much of this was just Brigitte's way, and how much was her subconscious realizing he wasn't an ordinary cat.

He purred, butting his head against the bottom of her chin.

"Look," she said, carrying him toward her desk. "You have your own special tree right here." She gestured to a floor-to-ceiling cat playhouse beside the desk, not far from the computer. The

20

colors of carpet and fabric complemented the room and the curtains.

He'd never gotten to play with cat toys or scratching posts; his father didn't believe in indulging his cat side. It looked new, but smelt like it belonged here. He watched, attentive as she patted each level, pointing out the perches and nice things to rub against. This was clearly not some random item purchased at a pet supply store. It was either made to order, or designed and made by his witch herself. The possibility that she'd put this kind of thought into her preparations for her familiar made his breath catch in awe. He wasn't merely an animal used to boost and focus her magic. Already, she valued him far more than his father ever had.

"And here you have a kitty hammock." A net of pink denim, a perfect match for her pants from the other day, hung over the edge of the desk. "I was thinking it might be a good place to nap while I do my homework." She leaned forward and encouraged him to climb onto one of the observation platforms.

The carpeting was soft under his paws. He tentatively batted at one of the walls, engaging his claws briefly. They sank in and caught nicely, satisfying his urge to grab and yank things. He peeked into a large tube and saw a stuffed toy dangling from the ceiling. It made a sweet soft jingling sound when he struck it.

"Oh, yeah," she said, watching him. "We can switch the toys out if you don't like any of them, or if you want to move them around."

He glanced at her over his shoulder then continued his investigation of the structure he was now certain she'd made.

"You enjoy yourself," she said, sounding pleased. "I really want to spend some time with you, but I have to finish my schoolwork first." He heard her rummaging in her backpack. "Physics was easy today, so I'll start with that..."

While she worked her way through the day's assignments, he

finished his exploration, eventually moving into the sling. It was quite comfortable, supporting his body while allowing him to droop in the boneless way cats could. He could already tell this would be the perfect spot to be near her while she studied. Every so often she'd look up and smile at him, giving him gentle pats and praise each time. He could see this developing into a nice routine for them.

* * *

"You've been so good and patient," Brigitte said, reaching out to run a hand along his side. "Just one class left. It's not my best subject, so I hope you can bear with me." She'd started Mandarin last year. Part of her regretted not taking Italian or German like her friends Ruhul and Aalia. At least they shared the same alphabet as French. But when it was time to pick classes, Mandarin was a new option. Though her mother had never pushed her to connect with her heritage, she felt compelled. After all, Ruhul spoke Arabic at home, and Aalia spoke Antillean Creole with her family.

Pulling out a hanzi grid, she slowly and carefully drew her characters for the day, focusing on putting down each line and dot in order. Her handwriting was decent, but her pronunciation was hideous. She was best at differentiating the tones if people spoke slowly, but most of the time it was a jumbled mess.

"*Wǒ... shì... fǎ guó... rén,*" she said slowly, her finger under the characters on the page. While she was repeating this week's phrases for memorization, Hēi Māo leaned over, gracefully spilling out of his hammock onto her desk. He padded over and looked down at the page.

"*Nǐ hǎo,* Hēi Māo," she said happily. "Do you speak Mandarin?"

In response, he reached out and pressed his paw on the page, dragging it away from her. She would have assumed he was bored and playing with it, but he'd turned it so he could look at it

22

right way up instead of sideways. His head tilted, and he let out a long rolling, "Miaowww."

"I know," she agreed. "It's not very impressive, but it's only my second year. And I'm not the worst in the class."

"Rrrrrrr." A low hum came from the back of his throat, like he was musing aloud. He reached out again and pulled her hanzi grid toward him. He tapped just off to the side of one row.

"You like that one?" she asked, grinning at him. "You should. It means cat."

He tapped it again, more firmly, and looked at her.

"*Māo*?" she asked.

His tail swished gently as he stared at her for a moment. He tapped next to another character, the masculine form of 'you.'

"*Nǐ*," she said, more puzzled.

He returned to the phrase sheet and put both paws down on one sentence, only letting one character show between them.

"*Shì*." To be. "You are," she translated. "You are what?" There was no way this was an accident. The stray cat she was hoping to become her familiar could read simplified Mandarin characters as easily as he seemed to understand French.

"Meh," he called her to attention, the next character between his front paws.

"*Wǒ*," she said obediently. "*Nǐ shì wǒ*... you are me?"

He let out a delicate sniff as he scanned the pages, finally settling on the possessive article that turned 'me' into 'my.' Once she'd said it, he wasted no time returning to the first character.

"*Māo*," she said, noticing that he'd sat down, clearly done. "*Nǐ shì wǒ de māo*. You are my cat!" She spoke aloud as she translated, gasping as the meaning hit once the words were out of her mouth. He hadn't made it a question, but a statement. She clutched at the front over her shirt, over her heart. "You're my cat?" she asked quietly, her eyes starting to sting. "Really?"

He took a few steps closer so he could sit up and put his front paws on her shoulder. He rubbed his jaw along hers, as if clear up any confusion.

Chapter Six

The apartment was quiet, and Brigitte was peacefully asleep. She looked so calm and comfortable. Hēi Māo reluctantly left the warmth of her bed, hopping down to her desk before relaxing and letting himself shift. He sat in silence for a moment, hoping the green flash of his transformation wasn't enough to wake her. His old clothes were snug, though they were still in good shape; he'd not had the chance to wear them out since he ran away. While he planned to primarily stay cat, he'd have to replace the clothes for times like this, when he needed proper hands. Despite his limited socialization, he was fully aware that it would be creepy to sit around naked in a teenage girl's room, whether she was aware of him or not. But he could worry about clothes after he convinced her he was her familiar.

He moved on silent bare feet to her desk and rummaged quickly for the supplies he needed. He'd seen everything earlier. Scissors and note cards in the second drawer. Colored pens and pencils in the canister on her desk. Ruler tucked in the center drawer. He pulled out her Chinese homework and started with this week's characters. Using his neatest handwriting, he wrote out flash cards, hanzi on one side and pinyin with the definition in French on the other. His witch was so clever. With the right tools, she was going to pick this up and do great, and that's where he could help out.

While he worked, he considered what it would mean to be Brigitte's familiar. His witch was the sweetest person on the planet. As Jacque Parenteau, he'd met a good many people at photo shoots, galas, shows, pretty much any time his father wanted to parade him about. None of them were like her or her parents. They were so warm and kind. Even though her parents avoided touching him, they spoke about him and to him with more respect than anyone ever had, except maybe his mother. And **they** thought he was **just** a cat.

Brigitte made sure he felt welcome and comfortable, even though she seemed unsure about keeping him. She was so considerate. He just needed to convince her, because his mind had been made up before he'd first let her see him. Miss Gigi was right, and now that he was here, he understood better. **This** was where he belonged, even if he never revealed his other side. He felt happier here than he'd ever been. He could be truly useful here. He'd also be protected from his father's magic, so it was a win for both of them.

The bond was unbreakable, even non-witch-born knew that, and his father couldn't force him to go back, even if he were found. His new role would also give him purpose, something his life had always lacked. He nodded, refocusing his attention on the task at hand. He would do whatever he had to, to prove himself worthy of her. And once he had, he was determined to be the very best familiar in all of Paris.

He could feel the approaching dawn by the time he finished up. He suspected her parents would be up soon, and he didn't want to risk getting caught like this; all his new plans would be out the window before his witch woke, if that happened. He stacked the flashcards neatly on her desk, proud of his night's efforts. He'd managed to make flashcards for every week of the fall semester plus much of the second semester from the previous year. It helped that she was so organized and kept everything where he could easily find it. He shifted back into his cat form to return to the warmth of the bed.

He was Hēi Māo now.

* * *

Brigitte woke to Hēi Māo curled next to her head. She beamed at him. "You weren't just a dream." She caressed him lightly, loathe to disturb him if he was tired. She had no idea what the life of a stray was truly like, but she suspected it was exhausting.

He purred in agreement, but didn't fully rouse. When she started gathering up her school things, she found a pile of homemade Mandarin flashcards. A perfect character on one side with the pinyin pronunciation and definition on the other. The tidy handwriting was completely unknown to her.

"Yes. Of course," she said quietly, both surprised, yet somehow not. "If you can speak Mandarin, why **wouldn't** you be able make beautiful flashcards overnight?"

He didn't respond. Her kitty was sound asleep on her pillow.

Papa was at the table when she sat down for breakfast. Maman was downstairs running the shop and mixing up potions that needed morning attention, while Papa was between bread batches, with all the ovens full. Knowing their routines meant she was fully aware that she was at least ten minutes behind schedule and needed to pick up the pace or she'd be late.

"Hēi Māo says he's my cat," she said, taking her seat.

"We saw him tell you that yesterday," her papa pointed out as

27

he reached for a croissant. "That pawing and purring was cat for, 'you are my favorite person ever.'"

"Yeah, well, while I was doing homework he also told me in Mandarin." She pulled the flash cards out of her pocket and set them on the table.

"Your familiar speaks Mandarin?" He glanced at her in surprise.

She rocked her head from side to side. "Well he didn't **speak** it. He still has kitty vocal chords, but he pointed out the characters, in order, and scent marked me after I translated it."

Her papa beamed at her. "And **you** were afraid you wouldn't find a cat. That this one wouldn't want to stay."

"But isn't it a bit... unusual?" she asked. "Could Callie read before your ceremony?"

He shook his head. "No, but Callie was a regular cat. And while calicos are sought after, they don't have some of the innate abilities and magic their black kin have." He slathered his pastry with lingonberry jam.

"Can Callie write in French?" Brigitte asked. She'd seen her parents' familiar read over their shoulders. Sometimes she pointed out notations in spells, or recipes.

"No," her papa laughed. "Cat paws aren't designed for that."

Brigitte handed her papa the top flashcard. "Hēi Māo made these for me last night."

The amusement faded, leaving awe in its place. "Wow. That's... that blows my expectations out of the water." He ran his index finger across the French translation, then handed it back. "He must be exceptionally gifted, even for a black cat. Are you going to make it official?"

Nervously gnawing on her lip, Brigitte shook her head.

"He told you, very clearly, that he's yours, right?" Papa asked, his voice gentle.

She nodded.

"He's a smart cat, Cupcake. Given what you've learned and seen from him already, I can't see this as a mistake. He knows what he's getting into, and he's letting you know he's okay with it." He gently tugged one of her braids. "With him as your familiar, you're going to be capable of so much. Don't let go of that opportunity, just because he's different. I know you want to do this right, and I support that. But don't let uncertainty become an excuse."

Chapter Seven

Brigitte led her two best friends up the stairs to her room. With her hand on the door, she glanced back at Ruhul. "You sure Juniper will be okay with him?"

The boy grinned and reached up to pat the small red fox perched on his shoulder. "She's awesome with regular cats and even better with familiars. I don't think it'll be a problem. And if it is, she can go downstairs while we hang out. She's pals with Callie."

She nodded and pushed the door open. "*Nǐ hǎo ma*, Hēi Māo," she called. He'd woken up for pets when she'd been home for lunch, and he'd seemed interested when she told him Friday night was usually game night.

"You talk to him in Chinese?" Aalia asked. "Ru, do you talk to Juniper in Italian?"

Ruhul laughed and shook his head. "No. It hadn't even occurred to me to try." He followed the girls into the room. "How did you find a multilingual familiar, Gitte?"

"Luck?" she suggested peeking into the hidey-holes of the cat tree. "Where are you kitty?"

A soft questioning, "Mow," came from her bed, but he wasn't

30

peeking over the side yet.

"He really likes my bed." She wandered over to the ladder.

"With as much as your pops says he likes you, that's not a surprise," Ruhul said. "It probably smells like you, so it keeps him company when you're gone."

"Hey there sweetie," Brigitte said, smiling at the black cat sprawled on her pillow. "We have company, and they'd like to meet you." She thought for a moment, working through the translation. "*Tā men shì wǒ de péng you.*" They are my friends.

Ruhul laughed. "Juniper came from Russia. Maybe I should try Duolingo for Russian and see if she still understands it." It was a Moroccan custom to pair witch children with their familiars young, so he'd been the first in the class, at just over eleven, to show up at school with a clingy new familiar. He was always the first to help each of their witch-born friends as they adjusted to their new bonds.

"Oh my god, Gitte," Aalia squealed as Hēi Māo crawled into Brigitte's arms. "He's **adorable**." She started to reach out, but caught herself before she could be corrected. "Sorry. Still getting used to that." Aalia's family weren't witches; Brigitte and Ruhul were her first magic friends when she'd moved to Paris from Martinique eight months ago.

Hēi Māo stretched his neck to sniff at the other girl, then the boy. His head tilted slightly as he took in the curious fox. He wiggled a bit, and when Brigitte loosened her hold, he climbed up onto her shoulder as if in imitation of Juniper.

"Gitte," Ruhul said, puzzled as he stared at the cat. "I thought you said you hadn't gone through the familiar ceremony yet."

"We haven't." She put one hand behind Hēi Māo to keep him steady as she climbed down the ladder.

Ruhul snorted. "You look claimed by each other. It's a little fainter than most familiar bonds," he clarified. "But that's pretty common at first." He narrowed his eyes a moment and shook his head. "Any prior claim you thought he had is completely gone."

"What does that mean?" Aalia asked.

"Short story, that cat is definitely **hers**, no take backsies," he explained. "Long story, he probably has some magic of his own, and he's not waiting for her to choose him. He's made up his mind and he's made himself her familiar." He squinted again. "It's a little one-sided, yet. Probably 'cause Gitte hasn't gone through the formalities."

Later, the friends sat side by side on the chaise, which had been dragged over to Brigitte's computer desk. They'd already gone through Mario Kart, with Aalia surprising them all by being the overall victor for a change, and Brigitte couldn't bring herself to care.

"She's distracted by her kitty," Aalia insisted, pointing at Hēi Māo. "But I'll take it."

Ruhul laughed, his smile soft with reminiscence. "Yeah. That happens to all of us."

"What does?" Aalia asked.

"It's an adjustment to have a familiar, someone so connected to you." He reached out catch Juniper's muzzle in a gentle caress. "It's really nice, knowing you'll never be alone. I mean, you have to fuck up pretty badly for your familiar to snub you, and very few witch-born are willing to risk that."

"Does that mean her grades are going to slip?" Aalia asked, frowning a little.

"Teachers at L'Étoile du Nord are pretty good about accommodating new witch and familiar pairs," Ruhul said, glancing up for a moment before focusing on the racetrack again. "You haven't really gotten to see it, because most of us had ours before you moved here."

"But I've seen all the animals in class," Aalia pointed out. A full half of their class were witch-born and a few others had different forms of magical power or abilities. "How long does it take to get used to being connected to... someone like that?"

"It's usually just a couple of weeks," Ruhul assured her. "Gitte will be back in usual form soon."

"Gitte," Aalia said once she'd crossed yet another finish line in first place. "I know you've been focused on your kitty search, but did you see the update on the case with Jacque Parenteau?"

Brigitte felt Hēi Māo go still under her fingers. The famous model, son of her favorite designer, was right around their age. The consistently brilliant showings of the Parenteau fashion house was part of what first sparked her interest in design. She religiously followed their trends and news, and had been about ten when Pierre's wife vanished under mysterious circumstances. Normally she'd be more invested in this particular case; she'd actually kept tabs on it since Jacque went missing from a photo shoot at Grand Palais in June.

"Uh, no. Did they find him?" Brigitte asked.

Aalia shook her head. "No, but apparently they've had some good leads. Pierre announced that he'd received solid evidence to suggest Jacque was fine, and he seemed convinced he'd be home soon." She tapped at her chin with one finger. "He didn't say if it was normal evidence like photos or a letter, or if he was working with a psychic. But based on how he practically begged Jacque to come home, I'd guess he got intel that Jacque isn't being held anywhere against his will."

Hēi Māo's tail lashed about, and Brigitte settled a hand on him to calm him. "I hope he really is okay. I hate to think of all the awful things that could've happened to him."

Aalia patted her back, careful not to brush against the fidgeting kitty. "Remember, what we talked about Gitte. If the really horrible things had happened, there would've been a ransom demand."

Brigitte nodded. "I know. I just… I think he's had a difficult life, and I worry." Hēi Māo chose that moment to rest his head on top of hers, his little kitty motor vibrating against her scalp. She sighed, soothed by his actions.

When they switched over to SkullGirls, the black cat let out a couple of excited chirps and wriggled on Brigitte's shoulder. "You like this game, Kitty?" she asked.

He leaned against her and hummed.

"Come here," she said, patting her lap. "You can help me."

"You don't need help," Ruhul said with a laugh. "We don't even to try to beat you anymore. We just aim for as high a score as possible against you."

"No, no," Aalia said eagerly. "Let the cat help." She grinned. "He might even things out a bit."

Ruhul nodded quickly. "I mean, yeah. Please help Gitte out, Hēi Māo. As much as you want. She **needs** it."

"Hey!" Brigitte objected with a giggle. "We're still new at being a team, no judging."

"We aren't judging, girl," Aalia insisted, her hands out in a warding off gesture. "We're supporting your new relationship. That's what friends do." She ruined her serious statement with a laugh.

"Yeah," Ruhul agreed. "What Aalia said."

Brigitte settled her hand on the right side of the controller, her fingers hovering over the buttons. Wrapping her arm around Hēi Māo, she used her left hand to pin the controller to her knee. She pointed to the big gray buttons. "You're in charge of those, okay."

The black cat butted his head against the bottom of her chin and reached out to place his left paw over his buttons.

"Do we get a warm up round?" Brigitte looked up to find her friends staring at her, their eyes wide. "What?"

"Your cat plays video games?" Aalia asked, stunned.

"Ummm…" Brigitte took in Hēi Māo's gaze, intent on the

monitor, his lithe body tense and ready to leap into action. "No idea."

"I'm no longer sure this was a good idea," Ruhul muttered.

"How good can they **really** be at it?" Aalia asked. "They've never teamed up before, and it's not like normal teams where they each have their own controller." She snickered. "I kind of want to see what would happen if we gave Hēi Māo his own controller."

Ruhul shook his head. "Something tells me you're about to get schooled in the power of familiars, Aalia." He patted her shoulder. "It's okay though. I get to play the loser."

* * *

Hēi Māo liked Brigitte's friends. They were funny and kind to his witch, something that pleased him. Aalia spoke to him as though he were one of them, and he enjoyed the way Ruhul treated him, like he was an extension of his witch. His familiar, Juniper, was interesting, and he thought they could become friends in time, too.

He just needed to convince Brigitte that he was the best familiar for her. Helping her defeat Aalia and Ruhul at SkullGirls, while sharing a controller had been a ton of fun, and he felt it was encouraging her the right way.

He curled up on her pillow, purring as she lay down beside him, one hand slowly passing over his smooth fur. Once she'd finally fallen asleep, he crept out through the skylight. He lived here now, and he needed to fetch his few belongings. If nothing else, the money would allow him to pick up some clothes that fit when he needed his human shape.

The rooftop where he'd been storing his knapsack was several blocks away, a round trip he could manage in under an hour. Running back to the bakery in human form, with shoes that were too small, was uncomfortable. That feeling was only compounded by the fact that he was no longer used to being a human, but he simply couldn't carry the backpack as a cat. Getting his things up to Brigitte's roof took a bit of climbing, but he was good enough at that even as a human. He'd had a climbing wall in his old bedroom before he ran away, and her fire escape wasn't that far off the ground.

Once his things were tucked in a secure spot on the roof, he curled back up on top of Brigitte's comforter. He watched her sleep, listening to her soft breaths, before closing his own eyes. Perhaps tomorrow he could convince her that he should be her familiar. He appreciated her effort in letting him choose, but didn't she see he already had?

He'd met his father's familiar several times, of course, but she didn't like talking to him. She'd treated him as though his existence offended her in some way, like he wasn't human enough or cat enough. She loyally reported to his father, anyway, so it was probably for the best. Still, he'd learned enough to understand how these contracts worked. Living with the Defresne-Li family, even for a few days, made it clear that he couldn't possibly do better as a person or a stray.

Chapter Eight

Brigitte came up from breakfast Saturday morning to find Hēi Māo lounging on the rug in a patch of sun. Smiling at his obvious happiness, she slid his freshly filled water and food dishes into their spot, a corner near her sink, where they wouldn't get knocked over.

"I got you some nice salmon this morning," she said, thinking it might appeal to him. He lifted his head and gazed at her for a moment, before flopping onto his back and wriggling.

"Do you need company?" she asked, thinking it looked like a nice place to give him some attention.

He let out a plaintive and drawn out, "Miaow."

Giggling, she crawled over. He was extremely affectionate, continuing to choose pets over food. It only reinforced her thought that he'd been neglected in his last home. She ran her hand over his neck and behind his ears, scratching all the spots she'd cataloged as preferred or favorites. He wasn't going to want for attention with her, that was certain.

Once he started purring, she lay down on her side next to him, her hand still moving through his soft fur. His head was turned toward her, his striking eyes open.

"Are you happy here?" she asked softly, almost as if she were afraid of the answer. Everyone had told her he wanted to be here. Ruhul had seen a familiar bond between them, even without the ceremony. He'd told her himself that he was hers. It all seemed a little too good to be true. "I know it's only been a few days, but..."

A paw reached out and pressed against her mouth, soft with nails retracted. She knew if she tried to speak, she'd get a mouthful of fur. He tapped her lips twice as if to tell her to hush, before he pulled back the paw. He writhed closer to her, pressing his forehead to hers and closing his eyes. The light puffs of his breath brushed across her face, strangely soothing.

"I want to keep you, Hēi Māo, I really do." It was hard to explain this to him, but she had to try. "Even if you want to be a familiar, you just seem too good for me. I'm nothing special."

The rumble in his throat was a growl this time, not a purr. She felt he was more irritated with her self doubt, than her caution. But she shouldn't have been able to read him yet. None of that was supposed to come until after he formally became her familiar.

"You disagree?" she asked, half smiling at him.

His warm paw booped her nose, making her laugh.

"I know you think of yourself as mine." She reached over to scritch behind his ear. "I want to be yours, too."

His purr came back.

"A good witch is there for her familiar, for anything they need, to help them just as much as they help her," she explained. The relationship was intensely personal, despite the fact that part of it was always on obvious display. "I want to do that for you, Hēi Māo. I want to help you, too."

He booped her nose with his paw again. He followed up by reaching out, slowly and hesitantly, before plopping his paw down on her cheek. He dragged it back toward him, and for a brief moment she was certain he was petting her in return.

"Oh, you sweet, sweet kitty. I don't know where you came from or who hurt you..." She smiled when he cut her off again with a paw to the mouth. She gently caught his leg and kissed the center paw pad. "I know you don't want to talk about it." She ran a finger over his cheek, brushing back his whiskers for a moment. "I won't make you. But I need you to understand I'm here for you, too, okay? Being your witch means I have a responsibility to you, too."

Still purring, he nuzzled her face, that one paw back on her cheek again.

"Okay," she agreed. "I'll set up the circle before lunch. But there's one last thing I'll need to do, after our snuggle. I hope you don't mind sewing machines."

He pulled back a little and tilted his head, definitely curious.

"I need to make you a gift." She scooped him onto her chest and rolled to her back. "You'll see."

* * *

Respecting her request for privacy, Hēi Māo watched his witch work from his comfy hammock. She moved, snipped fabric, and ran her sewing machine with the smooth grace of significant practice. The slight whine before the machine fully engaged, and the hum as her needle did her bidding, were comforting. He'd heard these noises all his life, save for the last few months when he'd been on his own. He more than half-expected to find the sounds anxiety inducing, but they weren't.

Like his father, Brigitte was a designer, but it seemed that was where the similarity ended. Though he'd been in her life less than forty-eight hours, she'd shown him her latest sketches, welcoming his company when she worked. He'd never been allowed to watch his father, much less inhabit the same room while he was creating, even after he was old enough to stay out of the way.

"I'd tell you what I'm doing, but I don't want to spoil your surprise," she said, glancing over her shoulder to smile at him. "Normally, I'll let you watch if you want." Her cheerful promise emphasized her joy in creating things and her confidence in her abilities.

Were his father's dour nature and waspish behavior signs of self doubt? He sniffed. It seemed unlikely. As Jacque Parenteau the model, he'd met enough divas to know that some people simply thought they were better than everyone else, and seemed to make a game out of being obnoxious. His witch wasn't like that.

She measured out green embroidery thread, stitching with a swift and steady hand, while drawing her magic into the project. He didn't think his father knew how to combine his magic with his creations. As he thought about it, he realized it was more likely, that his father wasn't powerful enough to do it. At sixteen, his witch had more talent and skill than his father, and that idea pleased him greatly.

Chapter Nine

Hēi Māo met Callie last night, when the calico snuck into the room to assess him for herself. She'd been kind, assuring him that not all magic felt the same. She said that what he'd felt from his witch's power so far was what he could expect going forward. That it was comfortable meant they were compatible. She was almost as fond of Brigitte as he was, and she had the best stories about his witch's childhood.

Watching Brigitte set up her space for their ceremony was predictable, yet starkly different from his past experiences. His witch sat on a rug placed in the sunshine, not hidden away in a dark windowless room. Her altar was brightly cheerful, bedecked in red, and the candles marking the quarters stood on circles of bright colorful cloth. She had cautioned him about the fire, but had never once asked him to sit still and silent. She used no subtle or overt bindings.

* * *

Brigitte bent to place the last candle around her rug, marking the north point. "Okay, Hēi Māo. Can you join me in the center?"

While he'd left her to her work as she'd requested, his gaze had been drawn to her once she started preparing her casting space. He hopped down from his castle to sit in the center of the round rug, in front of her little altar, watching her. She wondered if he'd known he needed to be on that side, or if it had been luck. Either way, it was an auspicious start.

"Good Kitty," she said happily. "Remember, I don't want you too close to the candles." When she'd talked to him about the dangers of fire, he seemed unconcerned. Perhaps he'd been around candles in his old home. She lit the white miniature taper in her hands and bent down to the first candle, whispering under her breath. "I call the guardians of the east, masters of air and thought, to bear witness to this sacred contract." Walking inside the border of the circle, she bent to light the next candle. "I call the guardians of the south, masters of fire and perception, to bear witness to this sacred contract." She could feel the magic building in and around her, like a powerful static charge. As she straightened up from the third candle, she noticed that Hēi Māo had turned toward her, sitting calmly as he watched. "I call the guardians of the west, masters of water and love, to bear witness to this sacred contract." She stepped slowly toward the final candle. "I call the guardians of the north, masters of earth and empathy, to bear witness to this sacred contract."

With the last candle lit, she knelt at the west side of her altar, a wooden step stool that she had refinished and consecrated back when she was first learning magic. Unlike most European witches, she preferred to cast her long-form spells sitting on the floor, like her maman did. She held her little taper up, smiling at the cat across from her. "We stand outside of time and place, on the threshold of never and always to formalize and celebrate the bond between witch and familiar." She tucked her candle into the small holder on the end of the altar. The red altar cloth was clear aside from a handkerchief-sized square of cream muslin covering her gift. It was still a surprise, and she was both excited and nervous about presenting it.

Her palms felt heavy and hot from the magic gathering there, awaiting her bidding. Reaching into her pocket, she pulled out some dry catnip. With her other hand she lifted the square of muslin covering the green and black collar she'd spent most of the morning on. Crushing the herb between her thumb and fingertips, she sprinkled it over the collar.

* * *

When she'd closed the circle and her magic swelled inside, he felt calm, as he'd never been during his father's spells.

She lifted the fabric concealing her gift. "I give you this band as a symbol of our contract, and the promises I make to you today." With both hands, she lifted the collar and held it up, presenting it to him. "It has been imbued with charms and enchantments to protect you and keep you healthy. These magics will remain long after the collar wears out and returns to the earth."

He recognized the love she'd stitched into it. The quick release clasp, the symbols for his protection and health, and the pretty bell at the center had all been carefully chosen for him. He would be proud to wear it.

"Even when you aren't wearing the physical collar, it will be visible to those with the sight. It will inform others that you have been claimed by a witch." His tail curved and swished lightly, as he watched, intent on her words. She unwound a thinner, smaller band of leather from near the quick release clasp. "Likewise this wristlet will inform all others that I have been claimed by my familiar. It will ensure that all can see I belong to you." She held it out to him.

If he'd been in his other shape when she showed him her mimic of his collar, the symbol for all to see that she was owned by a familiar, he was sure he would have burst into tears. The emotion bubbling up in his chest compelled him to act. He leaned in and rubbed his scent into her wristlet.

She beamed at him as she buckled the mimic onto her left wrist. "In exchange for your companionship and arcane assistance, I pledge to care for you, to love you as my dearest companion, and to do my best to bring you a full and happy life."

He bowed his head, while she adorned him, her fingers trembling as she fastened the collar to be comfortable. It was a badge, not a tool of control, and he was honored to be worthy of it.

Raising both hands, she banished the circle. "Depart in peace, elemental guardians. We humbly thank you for your protection." As she dropped her hands, the candles all went out, thin wispy trails of smoke dancing and twisting over the wicks.

With the magic complete, he lightly placed his front paws up on the altar to lean toward her.

"There. Now you're really mine, and no one can take you away," she said, and he wondered if she somehow knew that was one of his fears. That he would be forced to leave this place of warmth and love.

He hopped into her lap, purring and nuzzling her. *Safe*, he thought to her, hoping she could hear him.

Chapter Ten

Hēi Māo settled himself on Brigitte's shoulder when she sat down for lunch. She could literally feel the pride and contentment radiating off him. There was no doubt in her mind now that he'd been angling to become her familiar from their first meeting, and he was pleased with the witch he'd chosen. She wasn't sure why he'd chosen her, but she was willing to accept the blessing.

"Brigitte were you still going to go shopping this afternoon?" Maman asked as she added finishing touches to the three plates on the counter before her. She'd offered to take her daughter's usual weekend tasks so she could spend time with her new kitty.

Brigitte glanced at the black cat and he leaned against her gently. *I go where you go,* his mind whispered to hers.

"Yeah." She was relieved he was willing to go out with their bond still so new, not all familiars were so comfortable right away. "I need a few things if I'm going to finish that project. Is there anything you need me to pick up?"

"Yes, if you…" Maman's words cut off as she turned and noticed Hēi Māo and his new collar. "Oh," she gasped. "You **did** do it. I thought I felt you summoning a ward, but you seemed determined to wait this out." Her voice was soft and reverent. "Oh sweetie, he's perfect for you, I can see it." A couple of tears leaked unnoticed down her cheeks. "And you, sir," she addressed Hēi Māo, "are most welcome to the family. I can't guarantee Niklas and I will always understand you, but you can tell Callie if there's anything you need, and she'll tell us."

"Thank you, Maman," Brigitte said, reaching up to run a hand down Hēi Māo's back. "You've made him happy."

"You can feel his emotions already?" Her maman looked surprised. "You're a fast learner," she told the cat.

"I think I could kind of feel them before the ceremony," Brigitte admitted. "And last night Ruhul said he could already see a familiar bond between us."

Her mother chuckled. "That kitty boy chose you, Gitte. He wasn't letting you get away."

* * *

She hadn't sent him thoughts yet, but based on her responses, she was getting his just fine. Callie had explained how witch and familiar links worked, and he was pleased to be better at it than a regular cat. Without much effort, he could feel how important her shopping trip was for her projects and how excited she was to work on them. He was eager to show off his wonderful witch, and an adventure with her seemed the perfect way to celebrate their new bond.

He enjoyed his first ever ride on the subway, nestled snugly in a little sling across Brigitte's abdomen. She explained that she made it so he could have privacy if he wanted, and blocking out some of the sounds and smells on public transit made it less overwhelming. It also kept them close.

Brigitte hadn't mentioned it, but Callie had explained that the family lost a familiar in a horrible attack many years ago. Brigitte probably didn't remember the cat or the event, but she'd grown up seeing her mother mourn on each anniversary. The loss had imprinted on her a need to keep him close and safe. Her hand strayed frequently into the opening to caress his back or scratch his neck. It was delightful, helping time pass quickly.

At the store, he watched as her fingers poked and stroked various materials before adding bolts and spools to her cart. The irony that Pierre Parenteau's missing son was visiting a fabric store was not lost on Hēi Māo. He'd never seen his father at any point in the creative process, but he suspected it wasn't the same effusive and joyful experience his witch was sharing with him. He climbed carefully to her shoulder, liking the vantage point of this perch. He sniffed at the fabrics as they passed, and watched as she contemplated each item before it went into her cart. She made notes on her phone, occasionally snapping a picture of something she was passing up.

* * *

"Good day, Brigitte," the shopkeeper called. "Working on another project, are you?"

"Hello Monsieur Gavel." She turned and waved across the store. Even when she was very young, accompanied by her mother to pick out fabric for her learning experiments, he'd always been kind. He seemed to know, even then, that she would be a loyal long-term customer if he treated her well. "I've actually got two in the works."

The squat little man navigated around the racks toward her. "Is there anything I can help you– oh bless me, you've found your familiar!" He beamed at her.

Brigitte couldn't prevent the gigantic return smile. She'd hoped he'd notice.

"Hello, sir," Monsieur Gavel said, speaking directly to Hēi

Māo. "You are a **very** handsome fellow." He met Brigitte's eyes. "And a black cat, at that. You lucky girl." His own familiar was an orange tabby with impeccable taste in ribbons. "Congratulations to you both."

"Thank you." Brigitte giggled as Hēi Māo's tail slipped around her neck, the tip lazily swishing to tickle her chin. "He's very special."

"I can see that," Monsieur Gavel agreed. "Have you found everything? Ready for me to start cutting?"

Brigitte nodded. "I need six of the black. I'm using it for two different projects. And three of the yellow." She held up a finger. "Oops. Still need some trim. I'll just bring that up when I find it."

"Sounds good," the shopkeeper agreed. "I'll get these going while you're at it."

* * *

His witch had stuffed her purchases into her knapsack, leaving her hands free, and his sling accessible. "You're looking a little drowsy, Kitty. Perhaps we should snuggle in the sun for a bit when we get home."

Between the magic earlier and their outing, he felt drained in a way he wasn't accustomed to. He purred and pressed his face into her hand, all in favor of the idea of a snuggle.

She boarded the subway, her fingers dancing lightly over his body while she talked to him. "I'm assembling a capelet, designed after the yellow swallowtail butterflies. There'll be a bit of embroidery for the veins and the orange dots at the tornus. If it turns out well, I'd like to make a whole line of them to sell on consignment or online. Scarabs, moths, even birds would work well. Maybe a peacock. Maman **loves** peacocks. I guess they were important to her mama, who was of the Dai People." She reached up and took hold of the overhead bar. "When I'm wearing it, it'll look like a butterfly with its wings open."

She was so creative! Did his father bounce ideas off anyone like this? Had he done this with Maman? Or did he hoard all the energy and enthusiasm for himself?

"That black fabric I got today is extra durable. I'm going to use it to reinforce the shoulders in case you keep those as favorite spots to perch on me."

Instead of discouraging him from a behavior that could be inconvenient, she was altering her design to accommodate him. He curled around her hand and purred overwhelmed by yet another show of her kindness.

Chapter Eleven

Hēi Māo rode to school in his sling, with his face peeking out. His witch had been a distracted mess this morning, her first day back at school with a bonded familiar. He couldn't help but feel a bit smug over her happiness and excitement as she darted around her room shoving things into her knapsack. She kept up a running monologue about her classes, her teachers, and the familiars he would meet.

He kept an eye on the time, giving gentle reminders to keep her moving until they were out the door.

School is very close, she told him. *It's easy to come home for lunch.*

Do we have lunch with friends? he asked.

She paused at the crosswalk and smiled down at him. "Sometimes. This week we're going home for lunch so you and I have a little calm time in the middle of the day just for us. But we'll probably go out to a cafe next week to celebrate us." She joined the crowd rushing across the street with the light. "Ruhul, Aalia and I like to do that. Celebrate each other."

Good friends! He couldn't imagine what it was like to have people in his life like that. Fortunately, he didn't have to imagine anymore, he was getting to live it. When they arrived at school, it looked nothing like he expected. Groups of students stood out front, talking and joking with each other. It was far less regimented and orderly than his father made school sound. It was also very loud, kind of like the audience at a fashion show. He heard Ruhul's voice over the din.

"Gitte! You're on time!" the boy called. "And do I spy a kitty sling there?"

Aalia's voice was an indistinct squeal.

"Oh come on you two," Brigitte replied. "Let's go in. I think the crowd out here is a bit much for his first look at things." Her hand slipped into the sling to slide over his back, soothing him.

Once she had placed her things in her locker, she loosened the sling and drew aside the top flap. He could still hide, safe in the folds of fabric, if he chose, but he could also get out more easily.

"Good morning Hēi Māo," Aalia said brightly. "Gitte and I share a desk for most of the day. Ruhul and Juniper will be sitting right in front of us, so you'll have friends all around you."

He looked at the brown-skinned girl and let out a little chirp. She was very considerate.

"You can come out whenever you're ready, little dude," Ruhul said, waving at him. "And Junie is here for you if you have any questions about school or rules or stuff."

"And if this is all a bit too much, I'm going to be wearing the sling all day," Brigitte said, patting the wide strap that covered her left shoulder to cross her body on both sides. "You can stay tucked away if you prefer."

There would be fewer kids in class than out front or in the hallways, he supposed. And it couldn't be any harder than their shopping trip. He squirmed out of the sling, using the strap as a path to her shoulder. He draped his tail around the back of her neck.

"I guess that answers that," Ruhul said with a bright smile. "Nice choice, dude. Juniper's a fan of shoulders too." He crouched down and extended a hand toward the red fox who was snuffling in the bottom of Brigitte's locker.

She leaned back and met Ruhul's eyes, then scampered up and across his arm to get to his shoulder where she let out a cheeky undulating cry. "School is for naps and interesting smells," the fox's words were clear to him, though he was sure he'd never learned to speak the language.

As Brigitte and her friends walked down the hall toward their classroom, Hēi Māo noticed other students pausing to stare at his witch and her new familiar. He straightened up, briefly reminded that appearances mattered to many people, or so he'd learned. He'd only cared before because his father would withhold favored foods or activities if he failed to present properly. Now, however, he was inspired to reflect well upon Brigitte. As she took her seat, the other students got bold, gathering around the table she shared with Aalia.

"Brigitte, did you get your familiar this weekend?" asked a tiny blonde dressed all in pink.

"I'd think that's pretty obvious, Rosie," deadpanned the taller girl holding her hand. Her long black hair was dyed purple at the ends, and it hung across her face concealing one eye. "Where'd you find him, Gitte?"

"He was a stray," Brigitte said. "And he picked me." She looked up into his face as he remained on her shoulder. "He's really smart, and such a sweetheart."

"He's beautiful," the tall girl said quietly. "Congratulations."

* * *

Brigitte was relieved when the bell rang, forcing her excited classmates to dissolve their swarm around her. Hēi Māo looked okay; his body language all said he was fine, but she could feel his unease in the crowds.

Don't worry. It's not normally this crazy. Sending or sharing specific thoughts in word form was still new, and she tended to forget it was an option most of the time.

"Madame LaMarr," Celeste called, unnecessarily raising her hand as she called the teacher's attention. "Defresne-Li has a filthy mangy stray in here, and I'm certain it hasn't been properly vetted." She scooped up the dark Siamese beside her, cuddling it against her chest as she flipped her luxurious blond ponytail over her shoulder. "She's putting **all** our familiars at risk."

There was a unified gasp of horror nearly instantly followed by sounds of rage from nearly all the other familiars in the room. Juniper snarled, her front paws coming up onto the table as she glared at the class bully. A moment later, the rest of the class joined in, even those who weren't witch-born.

"How dare you?"

"You do **not** insult another witch's familiar!"

"You stupid, jealous bitch!" Aalia shouted, leaping to her feet.

Brigitte felt a combination of delight and horror. It admittedly felt very nice to have so many friends come to her defense, but didn't they see they were only playing into Celeste's game? As the utterly spoiled, only child of the mayor of Paris, the blonde held political power over their teachers and her fellow students. Her frequent threats to call her father, to influence cuts to school funding, or send the appropriate regulators after her classmates' parents got her whatever she wanted, whenever she wanted it. She delighted in striking fear into those around her, and she toyed with people's feelings for entertainment.

"That is **quite** enough," Madame LaMarr said, her sharp voice cutting through the din. She looked furious as she turned to

Celeste. "Mademoiselle Marchand, I am certain that being raised in such a prominent public setting, you have been trained in appropriate etiquette."

Celeste had the gall to look affronted. "Of course I have, madame, but–"

"And as a familiar-bonded witch yourself," Madame LaMarr continued, running right over the girl's excuses. "You are surely aware that the ceremony cleanses communicable diseases and infections from the familiar."

Brigitte stared in awe. Madame LaMarr was one of the most beloved teachers in the school, usually resolving disagreements with compassion and a soothing voice. But apparently even she had her limits, and Celeste had found one of them.

"Anyone with the most infinitesimally small hint of the sight can see that, that black cat is Mademoiselle Defresne-Li's familiar." She took an audible breath and turned to look at Brigitte with a strained smile. "Would you care to introduce the class to your partner, or will you two need some time to recover from the intense emotions of the last few minutes?"

"**That** is **not** a familiar," Celeste sneered. "I heard her talking about it. It was a stray, and she probably picked it up from some filthy back alley in the Chinese Quarter." Her face twisted in revulsion.

Madame LaMarr couldn't have looked more shocked if Celeste had gotten up and slapped her.

Hēi Māo hopped lightly off Brigitte's shoulder to the table. His brilliant eyes glared at the blond girl as he strolled to the edge. He squinted a moment before letting out a drawn-out hiss. He flashed his teeth at her in a snap before turning his back on the girl in an obvious snub. He scampered back to Brigitte, brushing his cheeks against hers.

Don't listen to her, he whispered in her mind. *She's not worth your time.*

Brigitte wrapped her arms around him, cuddling him close as she fought down the queasiness and hurt. Celeste reserved her nastiest tricks for Brigitte, and it wasn't the sort of thing she could just get used to.

Madame LaMarr continued her object lesson. "And of course you paid attention during history and literature when we covered the fact that an animal's place of origin is not necessarily an indicator of its value or suitability as a familiar, did you not? Your essay on the subject showed remarkable compassion on the subject."

Celeste looked taken aback for a moment, clearly surprised to have to fight a teacher on this issue. "I've had time to rethink my position. And I don't want that disgusting creature or its equally vile halfbreed contaminating **my** learning environment."

"Very well, Mademoiselle Marchand," Madame LaMarr said tightly. "Your hostility toward your classmate's familiar and your derogatory remarks about her ethnicity have earned you a trip to the headmistress." It was probably the one line not even Celeste could cross without being penalized.

Celeste's eyes went wide. "When my father hears about this–" Her hand dived into her purse to pull out and flash her rhinestone-bedazzled cellphone.

Madame LaMarr took two steps and plucked the oft-brandished device from the girl's hand. "I very much look forward to a conversation with your father. I expect he will be dismayed by your openly racist and classist remarks." She moved to place the phone in her desk. "Do not keep the headmistress waiting."

Glowering darkly and muttering threats, Celeste stormed out of the room.

Brigitte was grateful for Madame LaMarr's actions. She just wasn't sure she could keep her emotions or magic under control in this situation, even if it was to be expected. Over time, what started as mocking had gotten worse, periodically crossing over into assault. But Celeste's father held too much sway over their headmistress and several of their teachers, so somehow Brigitte was the one who got the blame when she reported problems with the other girl. If it weren't for her friends, she would have switched schools long ago. She wasn't sure if today would represent a significant change in her teachers' reactions, but it seemed hopeful.

Madame LaMarr placed her hands together. "Now then class. I think we need to banish the unpleasant energy from our room before we can hope to have a productive morning. Please close your eyes and begin your breathing exercises."

Chapter Twelve

Brigitte started, erased and restarted her latest physics problem. It was her toughest class, next to Mandarin, and she felt her grasp of the subject matter slipping away as the semester progressed. The warm puddle of cat on her lap stirred and shifted, sitting up to look at her tablet.

"You can rest," she whispered, trying not to disturb her classmates during work time. During the lecture, her familiar sat attentive on her table, his head tilting a bit now and then. She probably should have tried to follow his example, but she'd been too distracted by how cute he was, paying attention in class. Celeste hadn't been back through all of literature or science, and she wondered if she dared hope that the bully would be out for the rest of the day.

Hēi Māo climbed back up onto the desk to scrutinize her tablet. After a moment, he reached out with one paw as if to point. *Velocity, not speed.*

Brigitte stared at him a moment. If a cat was to understand any subject, she supposed physics made the most sense, but she'd always assumed they had a more innate connection with it. Still,

Hēi Māo had been all full of surprises in the few days they'd been together, and she was inclined to listen to him. She reread the question, thinking about velocity. It made more sense, and after a moment of hesitation, she was able to work through the arithmetic.

She managed the in-class assignment with occasional corrections or nudges from her familiar. It felt nice to work together even on something so common and everyday. She finished the worksheet just as the bell rang, which meant she'd only have the assigned homework for later.

Hēi Māo looked around the room as a couple of her classmates left and a few who had been in her first class returned. *You stay again?*

Even in her mind, he sounded puzzled. "Oh, yes. This afternoon I have classes in other rooms. Art and Chinese aren't held in here."

Ruhul turned around. "Getting the feel for things, little buddy?"

"I think he's surprised that we don't all switch rooms at passing time," Brigitte said. "I know there are some schools that have tried that, but I like our model." She packed away the paper science homework and pulled out her text book. She looked back at Ruhul. "We're picking our marginalized project topics today, right?"

"I thought that was the plan," her friend replied. "I've got two really good ideas, so I need to decide on one.

"You still haven't picked?" Aalia asked, taking her seat beside Brigitte. "Hey Hēi Māo, did you like physics?"

"I think he did," Ruhul said with a grin. "He paid better attention than Gitte."

* * *

Once he picked Brigitte, he'd expected her to be his only real friend. That was one more than he'd had in years, and tied with the most friends he'd ever had. But Ruhul and Aalia showed him that even in cat form, he had other friends. *Good friends*, he said to his witch.

They are, she agreed. *I knew they'd like you, and I'm glad you like them, too.*

The bell rang again, and he realized there was a teacher at the front of the room. He was young and wore his black hair in a short ponytail. A black and white border collie followed him in and went to sit in the large pet bed in the corner beside the desk. Hēi Māo hadn't realized it was there, probably because the first two teachers didn't have obvious familiars.

"Settle in, class," he called out, clapping his hands twice. "We have a few things to go over before you submit your project proposals and start on research." He tapped something on his desk and the white board behind him came to life with the title page of a slide show already queued.

Marginalized Communities: Shape-Shifters in Europe

Hēi Māo's interest was piqued. This was a subject even more dear to him than physics.

"Awww," a boy groaned from the back of the room. "Monsieur Levale, we already understand the project. We don't need an example."

Monsieur Levale's eyebrows rose a bit. "While I appreciate that you have a grasp of the expectations of the project, Simon, that's not entirely why I'm showing you this." He looked out at the class. "Your projects will explore the prejudices and traditions of marginalized communities, ideally a wide range of them." He gestured to the board. "This is perhaps the most extreme example of marginalization on the planet, and my experience has shown how unlikely it is that any of you will choose this community. So it is my responsibility to ensure that you **see** this issue."

Hēi Māo puzzled over the teacher's words. Didn't there have

to be groups of shape-shifters somewhere for them to be considered a community? Were there other shape-shifters in Paris that he would have met by now if his maman hadn't gone missing? He suddenly felt ill when he realized that he technically should have had grandparents on his mother's side, though they'd never been mentioned, and at least one of them would have been a shape-shifter. Did he **have** a community he'd been kept utterly unaware of? He fidgeted anxiously.

"How many of you are aware that you've actually met a shape-shifter?" the teacher asked. A few hands went up. He nodded. "And how many of you personally know a shape-shifter well?" Half of those hands dropped. "The truth is that it's highly likely that you have all met and interacted with a shape-shifter at some point, and you just didn't know it."

Hēi Māo barely moved for the entire short presentation. Sure, he'd been aware of anti-shifter sentiment, Maman had worked with him to control his shifting to keep it secret from the household staff. While she embraced their ability, clearly loving their shared time in cat form, she'd been adamant that he tell no one what he was. After she vanished, his father had taken the secrecy to an entirely new level, using bought magic to prevent shifting. When Monsieur Levale wrapped up and bid his students to individually meet with him to propose their topics, Hēi Māo crawled back into his sling, disoriented and weary.

"You okay, Kitty?" she murmured, her hands quickly assisting him into the pouch, and one hand resting over his shoulder blades. He leaned against her for comfort. "Yeah, that was a sad lesson. But Monsieur Levale was right to show it. I didn't really **see** the issue before. And now, I probably can't unsee it." Her hand slid over his back, comforting while his mind buzzed.

Chapter Thirteen

Brigitte lived five blocks from school, and lunch at home had been her family's preferred pattern since her final year of *école élémentaire*. Sometimes she went to Aalia's or Ruhul's, or the three of them went to a cafe or food cart, but for this first week, she wanted to spend her lunchtime with just Hēi Māo. She was used to all the craziness involved with going to school, but he wasn't. She'd read and heard that the sounds, smells, crowd and schedule could all be stressful to a new familiar, and she needed to make that adjustment as easy on him as possible.

The were nearly home when the yelling started. Her head shot up, and she felt Hēi Māo shift in his sling, a low growl in his throat. Down at the next street corner, surrounded by a sickly yellow glow, and levitating several inches off the ground, was Celeste. Whether her father had sent someone to pick her up, or she'd been kept in the office for the morning, she clearly hadn't let go of her righteous anger and indignation.

"Brigitte Defresne-Li!" Celeste yelled, her magically enhanced voice shrill and harsh.

Brigitte knew Hēi Māo's ears were pinned back, and she tried to soothe him without looking away from the other girl. "What do you want, Celeste?" She tried to keep her voice as calm as possible, hoping to avoid making things worse if she could. Celeste usually limited her bullying to the hallways of school, because she was protected there, but this felt entirely different, unstable and more dangerous.

Witches weren't exactly rare, and Brigitte looked around hoping for help. Surely there was someone nearby strong enough to defuse an arcane temper tantrum.

"You think you're special just because you found a cat to bind to you." Celeste slowly floated closer, her blond hair spreading out and twisting in a breeze confined to the magical aura.

"I have found my familiar, yes," Brigitte agreed. Hēi Māo crawled out of his sling, using its fabric as claw-holds to climb back to his preferred perch.

"You've forced some poor black cat into your service," Celeste sneered.

Brigitte felt Hēi Māo's hair raising against her cheek as he arched his back and growled at the other girl. "He chose me," she corrected. "And he's not fond of you. So we'd both appreciate it if you could leave us alone. This doesn't have to become a whole big thing."

"Oh I think it does," Celeste snarled, raising her hands. "You should have known not to try to outshine **me.**"

"Crap." Brigitte pulled a paper sachet out of her pocket and cradled it in her palm, prepared to ignite it when necessary. The shield could be summoned instantly, but it was a stop-gap, used in the heat of the moment.

Celeste's hand shot out. The sachet burst into painless flames, and the shield absorbed the spoiled girl's magic before dissipating.

"Celeste, get a grip!" Brigitte snapped. "It's one thing to pick on me at school, but this is assault."

Celeste screamed and swung her other hand out, magic leaping off her. Brigitte braced herself for whatever mess her bully had to throw at her. Celeste was more about showy appearances than substantive spells, but there was a lot of rage and hate fueling her now.

* * *

Hēi Māo felt his witch stiffen. *Mine*, he thought, launching himself off Brigitte's shoulder to intercept the spell with his body.

"Nooo!" Brigitte screamed high and sharp; it hurt more than the magic. She caught him, dropping to her knees and cradling him to her chest. Her fingers were gentle and soothing on his face.

He couldn't see her very well, and his whole body ached, but he nuzzled her fingers and purred as loud as he could. He felt so tired and strangely out of breath.

"No, no, no," Brigitte whispered desperately. "Why did you do that?" she wailed.

Mine, he explained. *Keep safe*. He'd known that getting between two witches and that kind of magic could kill him, but if it kept her safe, he was content with it. He just wished he'd gotten to be with her a little longer.

"I will **not** allow it," Brigitte said firmly, extending one hand, her fingers spread wide, toward Celeste.

He closed his eyes, feeling his witch's magic gathering around him. He hoped he could remember this moment of contentment even after he left this plane. He didn't want to forget this.

* * *

Hēi Māo's bright green eyes were cloudy, and his muzzle shot with gray. Celeste had aged her precious familiar. He nuzzled her fingers, his purr wheezy and uneven. Usually familiars grew old along with their witches, their status granting them unnaturally long lives and good health, but now he was frail with age. She vaguely registered that the other girl seemed to have realized how badly she'd fucked up, but Brigitte didn't care. Regret wouldn't save her familiar. She felt the tendrils of Celeste's retreating magic, like strands of yarn. With a twist of her wrist, she wrapped the other girl's magic around her hand, grasped it, and gave a yank.

Brigitte closed her eyes and wove her own magic around the strands she'd stolen. "We **reject** that which was given in thoughtless anger," she whispered desperately, not caring that she'd catch hell for using improvised magic without a ward. There wasn't time. "And we take **back** that which was stolen by loving sacrifice." The magic flowed through her and into Hēi Māo. His purr grew more steady.

Before letting go of Celeste's magic, Brigitte knotted it. It wasn't a long term fix, but it would prevent Celeste from using it again until a professional could clip it.

Brigitte gasped and opened her eyes. Her dear sweet Hēi Māo had been restored to his gangly young state, his coat rich black and his eyes clear green. "Oh Kitty. Don't scare me like that. I almost lost you." He pressed his face into her neck, purring for her now.

Worth it.

When she finally looked up, she was shocked by the crowd that had gathered. Celeste was being handcuffed by a pair of officers while another talked with some of the bystanders.

"Are you okay, Brigitte?" A hand rested gently on her shoulder and she looked up. The young woman was a waitress at the cafe one door up. She was also a regular at the bakery. "Is your familiar going to be okay?"

Brigitte nodded and struggled to her feet. She felt so cold and groggy all of a sudden.

"I'm taking Brigitte home. I'll be back in a few minutes, and I'd be happy to talk to the police, then," the waitress called, her hand coming up under Brigitte's elbow.

"Sounds good," a woman replied.

"Come on, Brigitte," the waitress said gently. "Let's get you two home where your parents can take care of you." She wrapped her arm around Brigitte's shoulders. "You can talk to the police later, when you're not so upset."

Brigitte let herself be led away, still clutching the nuzzly purring Hēi Māo to her chest.

Chapter Fourteen

Trembling and queasy, Brigitte lay on her bed with Hēi Māo. She'd thrown up once she got home, and she wasn't convinced it wouldn't happen again. Her eyes kept watering, whether or not she was actively crying. The constant purring and occasional kneading of Hēi Māo's paws against her arm were the only things that brought any comfort.

"I'm sorry," her mother said, somewhere downstairs. She was in the apartment, not the bakery, because she'd wanted to keep an eye on her daughter. "She's not at all ready to talk about it." Her voice was firm and not remotely apologetic. "She's had quite a shock, as I'm sure you can imagine. She only formally bonded with Hēi Māo this weekend, and to nearly lose him, like this, in their first week..."

"I **do** understand, madame, and I'm sorry to have to intrude at all." Half of the Paris police force had some form of magic. Most units were combined to ensure they could handle all kinds of calls. "I'll leave you my card. Can you have her call when she's able to talk? We can meet here or talk on the phone, whatever will make it easiest."

Not wanting to hear any more, Brigitte curled into a tighter ball wrapped around Hēi Māo. He was recovering from his near death experience with a nap, though his affection didn't let up even when he slept. She slipped her hand between his front legs to cover his chest and cuddled a little closer.

* * *

Hēi Māo curled against his witch's side, purring. Their experience with Celeste's magic, Brigitte's counter curse, and the whole reality that he'd nearly died taking a hit for her was exhausting. But it was clearly worse for his witch. Even when she wasn't crying or throwing up, her eyes would randomly leak copious tears. Other than being there for her, he wasn't sure what else he could do.

Nik brought him juicy bits of chicken, holding the bowl up for him, rather than expecting Hēi Māo to leave the bed for his supper. "You're a good boy," he said. "You did more than anyone could have expected of a new familiar, even if you picked her and have understood her since the get-go."

"Mrrrrr." He wondered if Nik had any idea what he was.

The man's big hand settled on her trembling shoulder. "Oh my poor little Cupcake. Magical overload is horrible." Hēi Māo watched as he brushed her hair back from her face. "This is part of why we use wards and study our spells before we cast them."

Oh. **That** was why she was so much worse off than him. He wondered if there was a way for him to absorb some of that impact next time. As a familiar, he boosted her magic, made her stronger, and helped her direct the flow. Magic was chaos, and the best familiars were creatures of chaos. As a shape-shifter, he brought a bit extra to their partnership, and he was going to need to do some research on that matter.

Her father settled another blanket over her shivering body,

and his hand covered her forehead for a moment.

"Mow?" Hēi Māo asked quietly, climbing onto her. Without Brigitte or Callie to intercede, it was a little limiting to be only able to speak to her parents as a cat. He'd need to work on that.

"You take care of her," Nik said, surprising him by understanding enough. "She's yours now, you know, as much as you're hers. I'd hate for anything to happen to either of you."

"Mrrrow," Hēi Māo agreed. He draped himself over Brigitte, his legs dangling down either side, and his purr a steady rumble.

After the house went dark and silent, he transformed so he could wrap himself around her more thoroughly. It seemed to help, because her random whimpers eased off and eventually her trembling finally stopped. His witch had worked so hard today, she'd performed magic that brought him back from the edge of death, and in protecting her from the other girl's spell, he'd inadvertently hurt her more than he could have imagined. He'd have to do better.

She didn't stir again until the hazy hours between midnight and dawn. He could sense her exhaustion. "Sleep," he whispered, hoping she was groggy enough to not realize the words were spoken out loud rather than inside her head. "You're safe. Just sleep." He pressed against her back.

"Kitty?" she asked, disoriented and fumbling to get a hand out from under her blankets.

"Don't move," he suggested. "Just sleep. I'll watch over you." As he'd seen her father do to soothe her, he lightly brushed his fingers against her temple.

She hummed. "Thank you Kitty."

"I'll keep you safe," he murmured. "I'll protect you, like you protect me." He felt magic rise at his words, making them more of a vow, something he'd be accountable to.

* * *

He shifted back shortly before dawn, sleeping a few more hours as a cat before fully waking. He felt for her with his mind and nodded, satisfied. She'd be waking soon, and he needed to do something nice for her. She'd been unable to eat for most of the day yesterday, so she would wake hungry. He could help with that.

Carefully slipping out of bed, he padded silently down into to the apartment. Ling was making tea in the kitchen, probably staying near, in case her daughter needed something.

"Good morning, Hēi Māo," she said. "Are you hungry."

He was hungry, but that was less important than tending to his witch, and she could help him. He let out a low, "Mrrrrr," then leaped up onto the counter to eye the sweet buns on a plate. He sniffed them, careful not to touch. When the scent of lemon hit his nose, he let out a happy chirp. He looked back up at Brigitte's mother and pointed at the lemon bun with his paw.

Callie wandered in then. "What are you trying to do, little one?" she meowed.

Delighted to have an interpreter, he hopped down to eagerly greet the older familiar. He rubbed against her from cheek to flank before speaking. "My witch will need breakfast when she wakes. I can bring it to her."

Callie tilted her head. "You're hunting in the kitchen for a gift?"

His tail swished happily. "Yes. She will appreciate it more than a bird or mouse."

Callie sniffed. "This is true. Humans are odd."

Having lived as both, he could see both sides of the argument. "I want to bring her a lemon bun. With jam." He looked up at Brigitte's mother. "Can you ask her to help me?"

Callie sat still for a moment, and it quickly became clear that she'd spoken to her witch on his behalf.

"A lemon bun?" Ling asked, putting one on a small plate.

"What kind of jam do you think she'll like, Hēi Māo?"

He considered the request for a moment. He'd only had a few days to get to know his witch. "Raspberry," he told Callie.

There was another pause. "Raspberry is a good choice," Brigitte's mother agreed.

Callie spoke next. "How do you plan to bring this to her?"

"Can she put it in a paper bag? A small one?" he asked. He'd carried lots of small things in bags.

"Oh," Brigitte's mom said. "You are so clever."

When he finally carried the small waxed-paper bag up to Brigitte's room, he could sense her waking up.

There was a gasp from the loft, followed by a tentative, "Kitty?"

He chirped to let her know he was there, and a moment later she was peering down at him from her bed. He set down the bag and looked up at her. "Meow," he greeted before snatching up the bag again to approach the stairs. He walked across her blankets and dropped the bag in her lap feeling very pleased. "Mrrrrrow."

* * *

Brigitte looked at the little bag, one they used in the bakery for tiny bites and cookies. "Who's a sweet kitty?" she asked. While Callie was an elevated cat, a familiar to two witches, she still had a tendency to surprise her parents with unpleasant treasures. "Did you hunt this down for me?" she asked, pushing away her trepidation at the possibilities.

He stood up on his back feet, stretching up to brush his jaw against hers.

Taking a breath to steel herself, Brigitte opened the bag to see his first gift to her. She let out a happy sigh. "Oh, a lemon bun... with raspberry jam." She gave him a look. "Did you have help with this?"

70

He held out his paws as if to suggest that having no thumbs was problematic. *I picked. My plan.*

"Ooooh." If she was understanding correctly, he'd had help with the jam, and probably the bag, but it had otherwise been his idea. He'd picked the bun and the fruit. "How did you know I'd like this."

He preened a bit, tilting his sweet head coyly. *Clever kitty.*

She giggled. "Not just clever," she corrected. "**Best** kitty, ever." She leaned forward and kissed him between the ears. "You're so sweet. Thank you."

Chapter Fifteen

While his witch was definitely better today, she was still exhausted and dizzy. He was more than content to encourage lounging and cuddles. Every time she sat down, he hopped into her lap, as if that would keep her there. She was also a little restless, having an odd mix of energy and apathy. But he was a shrewd kitty, and he had an idea.

After lunch, he darted for the stairs to her room. *Come with me*, he suggested. As he'd predicted, the sunbeam was lighting up the center of her room. He grabbed her blanket off the chaise, ignoring the unpleasant sensation of a mouthful of fabric, to drag it into the bright patch. Her slow footfalls on the stairs encouraged him to work faster. Back on the chaise, he used his hind feet to kick off a pillow. He was still arranging a snuggle space when she arrived.

What is this? she asked.

Come, he said. *Cuddles in sunshine.*

She sighed happily as she lay down in the sunny patch. "You're so good to me, my kitty."

He rubbed against her, then paused to peer into her face,

72

lightly touching his nose to hers. *You're mine,* he told her proudly. *Mine to take care of.*

She reached out, letting one finger gently stroke back his whiskers. "And **you** are mine to take care of."

Later, Hēi Māo gently butted his head against the underside of Brigitte's jaw. She was still drowsing in the nice sunny spot he'd arranged for them. Outwardly, she looked relaxed, but he knew better. Along their new familiar bond, he could feel tension and fear. He purred against her neck, rubbing his head vigorously all over her. Even in her sleepy state, she reached out and unerringly found him, her hand smoothing down his back. He loved pats. He'd gotten much more affection as a cat than he'd ever gotten as Jacque. It was so nice. He really would be content to stay a cat for the rest of his life if this was what it would be like.

He flopped onto his side so he could carefully knead his paws on her stomach. If she was going to give him sweet attention, he needed to reciprocate. Also, he was pretty sure he could feel her stress drop a little with the contact.

In the evening, when she spoke with the detective handling the incident with Celeste, he snuggled into her lap, using his purr help her make it through the interview. The man was nice, and he cared about justice. He'd seemed disappointed to reveal that Brigitte's incident with Celeste had made the major news. But he was quick to point out the good in this; the mayor would be unable to sweep the attack under the rug and get his daughter off, free of charges. The unfortunate bit was that someone had shared a cell phone video of the event online, and it had gone viral. Both Celeste and Brigitte had been identified, so she might end up with some undesirable publicity when she returned to school or went out for a while.

Although Hēi Māo hadn't been certain during class or the attack, the discussion provided enough information for him to verify he'd known Celeste as a child. She'd been the only authorized friend provided by his father. He snorted a little at the irony that his sole acceptable playmate nearly killed him. It wasn't much, but it was one more mark against his father's judgment.

* * *

With Brigitte sound asleep, Hēi Māo shifted into his human shape just long enough to get out through her skylight. He wanted to cheer up his witch, and he knew just the thing to do it. When Callie visited them earlier, she said that everyone liked flowers, and his witch was no exception. It was early autumn, but they hadn't had a frost yet, so he scampered until he found a park with flower beds that were still bright and healthy. Exposing one sharp claw, the one that lined up with his index finger, he carefully and strategically sliced through the stems. He made sure to spread out his clipping, so the gardens didn't appear damaged or unsightly.

He worked quickly, taking time to listen and smell the air, just to be sure he was still alone. This was his first solo outing since he'd bonded with Brigitte. He suspected Pierre wouldn't be able to find him now, but he wasn't one hundred percent sure. He just needed to be careful. When he looked down at the array of blooms, he sighed contentedly. There were more than he really needed, but that was okay. They weren't as fancy as the bouquets at his father's galas, but they were cheerful. These would surely help.

Working in his human form to take advantage of larger hands with thumbs, he gathered up the spoils of his municipal garden raid and hurried back home. He didn't want to risk Brigitte waking up alone. He crept back in through the skylight and set about separating the stems to create three separate bouquets. Three was a good number. He was pretty sure there was magic to be found in threes. Odd numbers were favored in Chinese traditions, as well, so it was perfect. Next, he found the right ribbons in her collection to tie them up. He was just finishing with them, placing them on her desk when he realized she hadn't finished her homework from Monday. She'd been in no shape for studies today.

A familiar helped his witch; he knew that before becoming one, and Callie had reinforced that philosophy. Nodding, he pulled her homework in front of him and got started.

Chapter Sixteen

It was Wednesday. She'd spent the entire day before lying around, feeling dizzy and drained after the mess with Celeste. She'd had enough energy to sit on the couch and draw, but that was about it. Some of her homework was incomplete, though she expected it to be excused given the circumstances, and she was still in her new familiar forgiveness period.

Sighing, Brigitte pushed aside her light blanket and climbed down from her loft, startled to find three fresh bouquets on her desk. Next to them sat the completed Chinese homework she hadn't gotten to before Aalia and Ruhul came over Friday night. Then she'd put it off in favor of time with Hēi Māo, expecting to have to rush through it over lunch. She stared for a moment, stunned. Her reverie was broken when her familiar bounded into the room, once again carrying a small bag from the bakery. When he saw her, he chirped happily and went to wind himself around her ankles a bit.

"Do you know where the flowers came from?" she asked, looking down at him.

Park, he replied in her head. *Pretty. Happy?*

"They **are** pretty," she agreed. One was tied with black

ribbon, another with green, and the last with red. "When did you do this?"

Early, early, early, he chanted, twisting around her some more.

"How did you do it?" That was really the more important question, and given that he was so chatty, she was hoping to get an answer.

Clever kitty. He hopped up onto her desk and set down the bag, his tail switching happily.

"The cleverest," she said, even if it wasn't proper grammar. She looked in the bag and found lemon bun this time with blueberry curd. "Do you know who did my homework?" She picked up the pages and noticed her physics assignment was completed as well.

I know. He padded lightly across the desk to rub against her face, one of his favorite places to scent her.

"Are you going to tell me?" she asked, stroking his back.

Ssssecret, he teased.

There were footsteps on the stairs, and Brigitte looked up to see her papa peeking into her room. "Ah. You **are** awake. I thought for sure Hēi Māo was mistaken." His smile was gentler than normal. "How do you feel today?"

Brigitte took a deep breath to assess and nodded. "I'm all right. Maybe a little tired, but really, not bad."

"Are you **sure** you're up for school?" Papa asked, crossing her room to take the other desk chair. "You can stay home today if you need to." He looked at Hēi Māo and then the other things on her desk. "Should I ask?" He gestured to the flowers.

Hēi Māo sat up proudly.

"He brought me flowers this morning. From the park," Brigitte said.

Her father looked at Hēi Māo for a long moment. "Your Mandarin speaking cat, who plays video games possibly as well as you, and who has taken to bringing you a breakfast bun in bed, gave you three separate bouquets."

Brigitte bit her lip, holding in a giggle, and nodded. "I think he may have done my homework, too. It's done, and I didn't do it, but he says it's a secret."

Her papa turned and stared at her. "Your familiar can do physics now?" He slapped his hands down on his thighs, before shooting Hēi Māo a mock scowl. "Over-achiever."

Yes.

Brigitte lost the battle with her laughter. "He agrees with you."

Her papa tapped her forehead with one finger. "Are you getting emotions or straight up conversation in there?"

She shrugged a little. "Shorter sentences most of the time," she admitted. "I started hearing words right after I gave him his collar."

Her papa let out a snort. "Most of us don't get words for months. Some familiars never branch out past emotional cues. I guess we should all prepare for the unexpected with your new kitty boy." He stood up. "So, you going to stay home or...?"

She could tell he was trying to leave her an out, make it easy for her to stay home if she wanted. "I'd like to try going to school. It's short day, so that should help. And if it's too much, I'll come home."

He nodded, resigned. "All right. But pay attention to your body and your magic, and know you can leave anytime. I'll go write you a note so it doesn't cause a problem if you need to get away."

"Thanks, Papa."

He turned to Hēi Māo. "And since my cupcake has notoriously poor self-awareness, I expect you to keep an eye on her and make her come home if she needs to."

Hēi Māo tilted his head adorably, then hopped into Brigitte's lap. *Yes. Mine to protect.*

Brigitte rolled her eyes. "Great. Now he thinks he's in

charge."

* * *

The day had gone well, but at night, the memory invaded her dreams. She was reliving Celeste's attack. Only this time Hēi Māo's heart stopped before she could save him. She was vaguely aware of someone gathering her close, and while it should have startled her, it was comforting, instead. She gasped when she realized she was in her darkened room, and it had all been a dream.

"Sssh," Hēi Māo whispered, his breath warm on her ear. "You're safe. I'm here."

"Kitty?" The endearment came out lengthened with a whine. "You died." She shivered and covered her face with her hands.

"No," he corrected. "You saved me." Soft fingers caressed her cheek. "You always save me." His purr seemed so much deeper and louder in the stillness of the night, vibrating her whole body just slightly. "It was just a nightmare. And I'm here to keep you safe."

* * *

It was just before dawn when Hēi Māo shifted on the corner of his witch's bed and once again pulled himself through the skylight. There was a hint of frost on the blue-gray rooftops this morning, which meant he needed to be careful if he went out and about as planned. His claws were fully engaged as he navigated to the sheltered space he'd hidden his backpack. Like many Parisian mansard roofs, this one had a completely flat top with shingles on the steeply pitched sides. But slick metal slopes were also quite common in this arrondissement, and his claws wouldn't prevent slipping at all there. He moved his bag to a more accessible location before opening it. Digging out the roll of money in its plastic bag, he pulled out a few bills before safely tucking the rest away. Yesterday's flowers had cheered her up, but she clearly needed something more potent, and he knew just the thing.

79

In his time as a stray, he'd frequently visited the alley of a Chinese acupuncture parlor not far away. The owner was kind, feeding him fresh fish and talking at length in both French and Mandarin. He seemed to know that Tom, as the man called him, wasn't **just** a cat, but it also hadn't bothered him. Even in his sheltered life as Jacque, he'd seen enough anti-shifter bias to recognize it wasn't exclusive to his father. But until Monday's fortuitous history lesson, he hadn't understood how pervasive it was. While he hated hiding things from his witch, he worried that revealing himself would ruin things. So he held off, disinclined to test his theory that Brigitte and those most important to her would accept him as he was.

Across from the acupuncture parlor there was a flower shop. He remembered it being open early, catering to those who wanted to surprise someone in the morning, and businesses that needed arrangements to positively influence meetings. He climbed down to the sidewalk, not wanting to risk the slippery rooftops, and scampered in the direction of the Chinese Quarter.

He was delighted to find he'd remembered correctly, and he darted into the alley to shift yet again, the green light washing over him. Living with Brigitte, it had become so easy to switch back and forth. From the shadows he watched, waiting until the florist flipped the sign from "Closed" to "Open." He pulled his hood up to cover his shaggy hair and hoped the florist and any of their staff or other customers wouldn't recognize the teen in ill-fitting clothes, even if his face had appeared on many billboards and kiosks around the city in the past. As a black cat, he didn't tend to have great quantities of good luck, but being with Brigitte seemed to have altered that. This new fortunate tendency held, and he managed to be the first customer of the day.

Hēi Māo looked through the selection of ready-made bouquets before requesting something special. His witch loved the color pink, so he found the blossoms that meant what he needed in pinks and whites, beaming as the florist arranged them, his hand waving over them to shower them with a boosting spell.

"That'll enhance the qualities a bit," the man explained, smiling. "Would it be all right with you if I take a picture of this?"

Hēi Māo took a small step backward in sudden fear. "What for?"

"I've not had requests for a healing and devotion arrangement before, which is honestly pretty silly," the man replied. His manner and scent suggested he was telling the truth. "I haven't even given it much thought, myself. But this turned out beautifully, and I'd like to offer something similar to my customers." He held up one hand. "But if you'd rather I not photograph yours, I understand."

Hēi Māo shook his head. "No, that's okay. I just... needed to be sure it was safe."

The florist took two photos with his cell phone before wrapping the bouquet in cellophane. "I wish your loved one a swift recovery," he said as he handed it across the counter.

Back home, Hēi Māo returned his change to his backpack before dropping carefully into his witch's room with her gift. As he was settling it on her desk, he heard noises from the kitchen. He smiled and shifted so he could fetch Brigitte breakfast again.

Brigitte's mother was not surprised to see him this time. "Good morning, Hēi Māo," she called, patting the counter. "Would you like to pick out Brigitte's breakfast again? I heard that it was very well received yesterday."

He chirped happily. Callie wasn't here, so they would have to make do without her, but Ling seemed intent on helping him. He pointed out the lemon bun again. It's scent and flavor were bright and cheerful, just what Brigitte needed. Ling placed the bread on a plate then turned to the refrigerator to pull out a tray. As she slid it onto the counter, he looked over the small jars of jam, considering.

He lightly tapped his paw on the lid of the cinnamon blueberry jam.

"You think she wants that one?" she asked.

"Miaow," he replied happily. This would be perfect.

"If you say so." At the sound of footsteps, she and Hēi Māo both turned to see Brigitte walking into the kitchen. "Oh, good morning sweetie. What have you there?"

Brigitte looked down at him, sitting on the counter, her eyebrows raised in question as she held out the bouquet. "Kitty, where did you get this?" He'd never heard that tone of voice, but everything in their bond told him she was worried about him, not angry **with** him.

He fidgeted eagerly on the counter. *Pretty magic.*

"It **is** pretty," she agreed. "Maman, he says it's magic."

Her mother held out her hands and took the bouquet, her fingers brushing the flowers lightly. Hēi Māo had heard of her talent for herbs and plants from Callie, but he hadn't gotten to see it in action. "Pink chrysanthemum for fidelity and optimism," she said. "He's a loyal kitty boy." She beamed, then continued. "White heather for protection and good luck. Hmm. He must be concerned for you."

"Is the last one mallow?" Brigitte asked.

Ling nodded. "Pink and white mallow, usually for healing." She looked into Brigitte's face, concerned. "Did something happen yesterday? Are you okay?"

Brigitte scooped him up, tilting her head the way he liked so he could rub against her neck and chin. "Yesterday was fine. A little exhausting. But Aalia and Ruhul assigned themselves my protectors, so I didn't have to deal with too many nosy questions." She smiled, relaxing with a sigh as Hēi Māo's purr started up. "But I had a nightmare last night, or maybe this morning. I don't remember it well, but I remember being scared, and he made me feel better."

Her mother found a vase in the cupboard. "This was made to

order," she said. "But I have no idea how he did it."

"How did you get me these flowers, you clever boy?" Brigitte asked, scratching behind his ears.

Not stolen, he said. *I have my ways.*

Chapter Seventeen

Hēi Māo was definitely the luckiest black cat in Paris, possibly the world.

He peeked out of his sling as Brigitte boarded the subway. As Jacque, he'd lived his life locked in a palatial room stocked with video games, movies, and books, because his father thought these would buy his cooperation. As if material objects were all it took to overlook his father's coldness and his mother's absence. He'd been allowed out only for photo shoots, and for those he was always escorted by his bodyguard. There was no dawdling or slow pointless strolling just to enjoy the buildings, the smells, the people.

He'd grown up in Paris, but felt he'd only started to get to know it once he ran away and lived on the streets.

Brigitte's hand slipped slowly into the sling to rest on his back, pulling him out of his introspection. *Are you okay?* she asked.

He rubbed his cheek against her hand. *I like this.* He liked everything about it. The sling and her proximity, the rumble of the train and the sway of her body as they left and approached stations. *I like going with you to see the city.*

She scratched lightly under his chin before moving her

fingers behind his left ear, a favorite spot that she'd discovered. *Well I like having you with me.*

For someone who had spent her first sixteen years without a familiar, she'd been pretty intent on not going anywhere without him now that they'd bonded. He spent time at school, learning along with her. He was especially fond of math, physics, and Mandarin. He accompanied her to the fabric store for the odds and ends needed for her current projects as well as supplies for her planned pieces. She was so busy, always making things, but she spent that time talking to him, maintaining a running narrative. At first he thought it was because she expected him to be afraid of her sewing machine. Now he thought it was just that she was kind, and didn't want him to feel excluded. It was so different from his father, who had used his design career as an excuse for the way he treated Jacque. Brigitte shared her drawings, asked for his opinion, and even accepted some of his suggestions despite the fact that he was a cat. His father wanted nothing to do with him most of the time, and Jacque regularly went weeks confined to his room without ever seeing the man.

Where are we going? he asked. Her school was on *les vacances de la Toussaint*, the two-week autumn break around All-Saints Day, and she'd been taking him to all sorts of interesting places in Paris. Aalia and Ruhul had been over yesterday to bake cookies and watch movies. *What is today's adventure?*

She smiled, and he felt her amusement. *Just going out for inspiration.*

Once she stepped off the train, he crawled out of the sling and up to the reinforced shoulder of her finished capelet. She'd been so pleased with how it turned out, and he could see the quality in her craftsmanship. It was an excellent choice for the sunny, nearly November day. There was a bite in the air, and he realized again that it was fortunate that he wouldn't have to winter-over as a stray.

"Are you happy up there?" she asked, reaching up to run her hand down his back. She wasn't afraid he'd fall, he could tell. She was just cuddly, and that suited him.

The view is good, he said, pleased with himself.

She snorted. "I'm not **that** short." She looked up at him as she grasped the handrail to ascend the stairs. "And I'm much taller than you."

Yes. And the view is better here. He looked into her face, leaning in to just lightly touch his nose to hers.

"Well someday I'll have to bring you up the Eiffel Tower," she suggested. "When it's warmer, of course. It has an even better view."

I've never been there. He'd been close to the Tower, posing for photos in it's shadow, but he'd never been allowed up. Unsupervised cats did not get to bypass admission, and he'd discovered that the hard way.

"Oh." She patted him again. "We'll definitely fix that."

* * *

Brigitte put the final touches on her sketch and glanced at her cell phone. "Time to head home," she told Hēi Māo as she tucked away her things. He was sitting beside her in a nest made of his sling and her black and yellow capelet, staring up at the Eiffel Tower. "Do you like it here?" she asked.

It's nice, he replied. *Less busy here.*

She nodded. Though they were starting to enter the off season, the Champ de Mars was still crowded with tourists. Her spot on the steps had a great view, but it wasn't as dramatic or highly recommended as other places. That meant it didn't draw tourists the way other locations did, and she could still look for inspiration among the people and pigeons of Paris in the shadow of the tower. "I usually come here a few times a month." She scratched his head for a moment and stood up. "There are a few other places I go, too. You'll see. I hope you like them, too."

Of course I will. He let out an almost indignant sniff but got up so she could drape the sling across her body. *I like seeing you happy.*

"You sweetheart." She swooped the butterfly capelet onto her shoulders, grinning as she watched the wings flare open. She was so happy with how it turned out. It was cheerful, and the way it draped over the sling allowed her familiar an extra layer of privacy in his carrier if he wanted it. The durable reinforcement fabric had worked just as she'd hoped; the old world swallowtail had black patches right where her shoulders were, and it matched up with his preferred perches. "Where do you want to ride?" Before he could answer, she felt the electric prickle of powerful magic in the air. It was like static, only stronger, vibrating against her skin.

Trouble! Hēi Māo could obviously feel it too, and his coat fluffed up in annoyance. Without warning, he leaped to her shoulder, his tail curving about her neck in a way that felt both protective and possessive.

Brigitte broke into a jog, intent on getting home as fast as possible. Her parents wouldn't want her involved in **whatever** this was. The Paris police force had an arcane emergency unit for this sort of thing, and she'd learned from an early age to seek shelter if things got dangerous. She heard the screaming and crashing of something a few blocks over.

This crisis didn't involve her. She just needed to keep safe until…

A woman with a stroller came running around the corner, heading down the street away from Brigitte. She was closely followed by a muted-yellow demon with periwinkle spots. It was probably twice as tall as Papa, which meant it was one of the older and stronger ones, and it must have gotten loose from whoever summoned it. Odds were pretty good that they didn't quite get what they were expecting and didn't have the power to contain or banish it.

She felt Hēi Māo's growl more than she heard it. "I know, Kitty," she whispered, her voice shaky. "But we have to help." The fight with Celeste had been the first indication of how strong her magic had become. The woman and baby's safety couldn't wait for someone else. She moved closer to the Seine's levy; she was going to need the extra help from water for this. She quickly shucked her shoes and socks, setting her bare feet shoulder width apart on the cold sidewalk. "Can you get its attention?" She bent her knees slightly; it was about to get rough.

Chapter Eighteen

On it. He bounded from her shoulder. He couldn't refuse her, because she was right. They had to help. But he desperately hoped he boosted her magic as much as Callie suggested when they talked in the wee hours. He let out a howling battle cry as he flew down the sidewalk, reaching the demon as it swiped at the woman.

Feeling strength from the rise of his witch's magic, he grew bold. He leaped onto the demon's leg, engaging his claws as he shot up the creature's body. He had its attention, but he needed to be sure it would abandon his chase for new quarry. He slashed one paw across its face, digging in with his claws before jumping off the demon's shoulder and racing back toward Brigitte.

Incoming! He warned, watching a breeze pick up around her.

Brigitte met his eyes before focusing on the creature chasing him. Swinging her hands in wide circles, his witch chanted. "With air, I confine thee. With fire, I bind thee. With water, I douse thy flame." The river rose up in a water spout that sprayed everything within forty-five meters. "And with earth, I crush thee." The demon staggered, unable to move forward or pull back. "You were brought here in error. You must go back."

It shrieked at her, flapping it's stubby wings and struggling against her binding. Though she held it fast, Hēi Māo could feel the magic draining her. This wasn't something she could sustain for long, and yet he didn't even hear emergency sirens, so no one was coming to help, not anytime soon.

Brigitte, his amazing witch, astounded him with her next action. "With air and fire, water and earth, I rescind your invitation, and banish you from this plane." She brought her hands together, her clap, a sharp crack of thunder. The demon vanished in a spiral of fire. A shock wave of wind shot out from the scorched sidewalk knocking Brigitte backward into the Seine.

Hēi Māo darted to the edge of the levy, frantically searching for her, feeling her rising panic as she thrashed beneath the surface. Shrieking into the link, desperate to find her, he immediately shifted and dived in after her.

He didn't notice the coldness of the river, his mind solely focused on finding her. His witch. His Brigitte. Their bond pulled him to her and he caught hold of her capelet to yank her into his arms. She was so still and limp as he pulled her out of the water. As she lay there on the cement he realized he was suddenly facing the potential of a world without her.

"No, no, no," he whispered, dropping to his knees beside her. "Brigitte?" He shook her, but she didn't respond, even in his head. He leaned over her, listening for breathing while two fingers searched for a pulse in her neck. He found neither.

Tipping back her head, he latched his mouth over hers and exhaled, watching her chest rise and fall. He repeated the breath then scrambled next to her torso, running two fingers down the center of her chest. Placing the heel of one hand where he felt her sternum, he set the other on top, locking his fingers together. "One, and two, and three, and four..." he whispered the count. He moved at the rapid pace he'd learned and practiced in a first aid course his father had found completely unnecessary but allowed anyway.

At thirty compressions, he started the cycle again with two breaths. He only got to seventeen compressions when she gasped and started choking. He rolled her onto her side in case she threw up. He was furious that there were still no sirens screaming through the air. He needed an ambulance. **Now.** They had to take care of his Brigitte. As she coughed and gagged, he fished in her bag for her phone. His witch was so smart and had spelled her backpack against water, probably because she had a tendency to forget her umbrella. Though he'd never used a cell phone, he'd watched her closely enough that he could figure it out.

"Emergency services," a calm woman answered. "What is the nature of your emergency?"

"There was a demon attack along the seine," he said quickly. "We need an ambulance."

"We've received a report about a demon in that area," the woman replied. "Ambulances will be dispatched as soon as the response team issues the all clear."

"We don't need a response team," he insisted. "My... a... a witch, she banished it. It's gone. But she fell in the river, and I don't think she can swim."

"Is she still in the river?" the woman asked quickly.

"No," he answered. Why was she asking questions? Why couldn't she just send the help? "I pulled her out." Brigitte made a horrible retching noise, as her lungs worked to evict the water that had gotten in. He patted her on the back.

"Is she breathing?" the operator asked.

"She is now," he answered.

"And the demon isn't there?" she asked again.

"No. It's gone. I told you. She banished it, and now she needs help. Please," he begged.

There was a moment of silence. "I've confirmed that the

ambulance is on its way."

"Thank you," he whispered, hanging up and turning his attention to his witch.

She was alive.

Chapter Nineteen

He was pretty sure he was crying as he rubbed her back.

"Kitty?" she whispered, once her breathing was steady.

He heaved a sigh of relief. She could talk! "I thought I'd lost you," he cried. "I can't lose you." He lightly caressed her cheek as he had when she had bad dreams. "Lie still, my Brigitte." He crouched over her, wanting nothing more than to bury his face in her hair. "Help is coming."

* * *

She remembered the siren and a blond boy with beautiful green eyes sitting in the ambulance, clinging to her hand. She was sure she'd seen him somewhere before. Then she was in a room that was too bright while someone examined her. A nurse was trying to make the boy leave.

"I'm not going anywhere," he insisted, his voice comforting, his hand tightly wrapped around hers. "I belong with Brigitte."

She closed her eyes for a moment, reaching for her familiar bond. She was horrified that she hadn't thought about it until now. But then she felt him **here**, felt that her magic and their bond were fine. Though she was still foggy and tired, her mind accepted all this; things that had puzzled her suddenly made sense. "Hēi Māo?" she asked, and all the other voices stopped.

The boy looked up, his wide eyes meeting hers.

"I need my kitty," she whispered on the verge of tears.

He was smart; he got the message. Squeezing her hand, he ran from the room.

* * *

Hēi Māo looked at the medical devices hooked up to Brigitte. He sniffed at the needle embedded in the inside of her elbow, but made no move to tug at it as a less educated familiar might. Her heart beat along with the monitor off to the side of the bed. She was curled on her side, so he snuggled in close, resting his head on her neck. The frantic purr that had kicked in as soon as he'd joined her in cat form had eased a little. Though the doctors wanted to keep her over night for monitoring, she wasn't at risk for severe complications.

Had this been what it felt like to her when he'd blocked Celeste's spell? The sheer mind-numbing terror of the possibility of a life without her had opened his eyes. His motivation to become her familiar had been driven by his own need for protection from his father. While he'd also seen it as a life where he could be fulfilled, that was secondary. Now that he was bound to Brigitte, and he'd seen that bond threatened, he knew nothing would matter if he lost her. He had a new respect for Ling's strength in not only carrying on after the death of her familiar, but managing to accept another eventually. He knew he did not have that resilience.

Being so close to his witch helped mask the pungent sterile smell of the hospital, but he couldn't rest. Everything was going to change, and he wasn't sure what he could do to make that go smoothly. Would she hate him? He didn't quite think so, though she would probably be disappointed, maybe hurt by his subterfuge.

His Brigitte was so smart. The way she'd looked directly at him when she demanded her kitty was enough. She knew, maybe not exactly **what** he was, but she knew that the boy who'd saved her was her Hēi Māo, her familiar. That was a bond that couldn't be broken or undone, and surely she wouldn't try to cast him out... would she? No. She was too kind. But would it ruin their partnership? What they had, though it was still new, was more than him just providing a magical boost. There was genuine affection and companionship, and that was the part he stood to lose now that she knew.

The door opened, and he smelled her parents as they quietly slipped into the room. Hēi Māo strained his eyes to watch them but didn't lift his head from its spot over her pulse. Ling reached out and lightly brushed her cheek while Nik gazed down at her, his worry and sadness palpable.

"Oh, Cupcake," he whispered. "What did you go and get tangled up in now?"

"Hello Hēi Māo," Ling said, reaching into the bag on her shoulder. She pulled out a container, and when she peeled open the lid, the scent of canned tuna hit the air.

It smelled good, but he closed his eyes and wriggled closer to his Brigitte.

Ling laughed a little. "Oh you sweet silly boy. You need to eat."

"Magic and healing are things that witches and familiars can help each other with," Nik explained. Hēi Māo opened his eyes to see the big man pick out a large chunk of meat with a pair of chopsticks. "The more energy you have, the faster she'll recover."

Oh. That made sense. It also explained why he was tired when she did big magical workings and why his napping helped her. His father had never explained those details. Why would he have?

Jacque wasn't the proper witch-born son he'd wanted, so he didn't need to know.

"Come on," Brigitte's papa coaxed. "Have a snack so you can help her."

Careful to stay in contact with her, he raised his head and slowly sat up. He stretched his head toward the tuna, opening his mouth when the big man brought the morsel closer. Hmmm. It was nice. Salty and tender. He'd eaten well since he'd first come home with Brigitte, and her family had quickly learned his favorites.

"There's a good lad," the man encouraged, drawing out another chunk of meat. "Have a bit more." He popped it neatly into Hēi Māo's open mouth. "No need to move. We'll bring it right to you."

As he chewed, he watched Ling comb back his witch's hair with her fingers. The strands were stiff and clumped, and he was sure she'd want a shower as soon as she was well enough to notice.

"Oh, my sweet girl," she said. "You rest. We'll sit watch for a bit."

"There you are," Nik said. "Last piece."

Hēi Māo licked the chopsticks as he caught the meat in his teeth. He realized that he did feel a little better, and he was grateful they were watching out for him. If there was a chance he could help Brigitte recover faster, he wanted to take it.

When he nuzzled her again, she rolled a little onto her back. Cautious of where he put his feet, he stepped onto her, curling into a tight ball on her upper chest and letting his purr do what it could for her. He was her familiar, no matter what happened next, and he was here to help her.

Chapter Twenty

Brigitte woke to an awareness of a gentle vibration on her chest. It was warm and soothing. The room was dim, and when she opened her eyes she found Hēi Māo curled on top of her, his black fur as silky as always. When she rocked her head to the side, she saw her parents, cuddled together on a loveseat in a room that wasn't her own.

Oh, yeah. She was in the hospital. "Maman?" she said, surprised by how scratchy her throat was.

Her papa opened his eyes first. "Hey. How are you feeling?" he asked, gently nudging his wife. "You breathing okay?"

She nodded.

"Warm enough?" he asked.

She nodded again, reaching a hand out from under the covers to rest it on Hēi Māo. "Sleepy," she mumbled. "Achy." She felt disoriented, her thoughts clouded.

"That's all to be expected," her maman said, getting up and pressing a hand to her forehead. "You had a rough afternoon."

"Get some sleep, Cupcake," her father said. "We're all watching over you.

* * *

Hēi Māo paced nervously on the bed as the nurse helped his witch to her feet. He was fully aware of, and utterly unable to hold back the high pitched growl he emanated, punctuated by anxious chirps.

Once she was fully upright, his Brigitte slowly turned her head to look at him. "I'm okay, Hēi Māo," she insisted. "But I feel disgusting and need a shower."

"I promise to take good care of her," the nurse said, smiling at him. "Your girl is in good hands." She wrapped an arm around Brigitte's waist and helped her shuffle slowly toward the bathroom. "Easy does it, Brigitte. There's no need to rush."

The nurse seemed nice enough, and he had nothing against her. She was surely quite skilled. But he didn't know her, and he would have felt a lot better entrusting his witch, in her fragile state, to her mother, her father, Ruhul or Aalia.

"Should I leave the door open for him to see you're okay?" the nurse asked. "I don't want to make him unduly anxious."

Brigitte nodded. *Will that make you feel better?* she asked him.

Yes, he replied immediately. *I won't peek.* He'd always been a model gentleman, turning his back while she changed and occupying himself when she was in the bathroom.

He felt her amusement. *I know. You never do.*

They hadn't talked about it yet, the fact that he wasn't exactly human, but there was no question in his mind that she knew. She'd been a little more closed off this morning, but not cold or withdrawn; it was more like she was puzzling through it and calmly accepting the way things were.

He listened as the nurse directed his Brigitte to hold on to the safety rail and sit on the shower chair. It was nice not to have to press his ear to the door to hear that everything was going well.

Brigitte enjoyed the warm water and the scalp massage that came from someone else washing her hair. He could completely relate to that. When the water cut out, he moved back to the bed to resume his pacing. He wanted nothing more than to rub up against his witch's ankles, reassuring himself that she was safe, while also giving her the affection he could. He'd briefly considered turning human, in case he could be of more help, but discarded the thought almost immediately. Being a boy had not been helpful yesterday; it nearly got him sent away.

The nurse dried her in the shower, helping her back into a hospital issue gown. "All right. Back to bed with you, my dear," the woman said. "The doctor is going to examine you shortly, probably before your breakfast arrives. I know she had you near the top of her morning rounds, right under the really critical patients."

Brigitte nodded. "Okay." She let out a tired sigh as she settled back onto the mattress.

"I suggest resting while you wait." She eased the blankets back over his witch, a gentle smile on her face. "Resting is your top priority right now."

Brigitte let out a little huff. "It's all I feel like, anyway."

The nurse nodded. "Not a surprise. Between the magic and the drowning, you have a lot of recovering to do." She looked at Hēi Māo. "You take care of her." She pointed to a red button on the panel behind the bed. "Hit this if she needs anything and is being too stubborn to ask for it herself."

He nodded, pleased to be addressed directly.

"When did my familiar become the boss of me?" Brigitte whined dramatically, grinning to show she didn't mean it.

"Didn't anyone warn you of that?" the nurse asked. "Once you belong to a cat, even one who isn't a familiar, they are in charge. They just let you think you're the boss once in a while." She laughed happily.

We take turns, he said, curling up between his witch's chest and chin as she lay on her side. *It's my turn right now. I will keep you safe.*

Brigitte moved just enough to settle her hand on him. *You're very good at it.*

* * *

By mid-morning Brigitte was eagerly hoping her doctor would give the order for her to go home. Even if she was just going to spend her day in bed, she wanted it to be her own bed. Her morning nurse Emily returned after breakfast, when Brigitte was feeding Hēi Māo bits of ham from her omelet.

"Oh goodness, he's a sweetie," Emily said. She was probably closing in on thirty, and her hair was up in a tidy bun. "Your parents are having one last word with the doctor, but they gave me your clothes, and I'm here to help if you need it."

"I might need it with the shirt," she admitted. "I know they said my ribs were only bruised, but... wow."

Emily nodded sympathetically. "And I hate to tell you this, but you're going to be pretty sore for a couple of weeks."

Hēi Māo slipped down to the floor and under the bed, and Brigitte smiled at his subtle attempt to respect her modesty. He'd always stayed out of her way when she was changing or bathing. She hadn't realized how odd that really was, and it should have tipped her off that he wasn't what he seemed. Her familiar was a teen heartthrob and actual supermodel. And he'd **chosen her** for a life-long contract. She suspected the pain medication was the only reason she wasn't completely freaking out, and she hoped she wasn't transmitting any of her mental gibbering at him.

She winced as she raised her hands to go into her shirt. Even the position, without exertion, hurt.

"I recommend button-downs for a bit," Emily said, smoothing down the back of the shirt.

"Yeah. Good idea."

"Has anyone told you about what happened yesterday?"
Emily asked.

Brigitte shook her head. "There hasn't really been the
opportunity."

"I figured." She helped Brigitte into a comfy pair of elastic
waist pants. "Do you want to know?" She held up a hairbrush that
had also been in the bag from her parents.

"Yes please." She reached for the brush, pleased to note that
Hēi Māo had come back up onto the bed now that she was
dressed. "Thank you, cl – uh, Kitty." She finished lamely. It felt weird
to call him a clever boy, one of her favorite names for him, knowing
that he wasn't **just** a cat. But by the same token, her family was so
fond of nicknames and endearments, and he'd seemed to like it.

He rubbed against her chest, pushing his face into her neck.
I make you happy, now.

Brigitte giggled. Maybe she didn't have to change her
reactions to him just yet. It was definitely something they would
need to talk about. "Yes, you make me happy, sweet Kitty." She
could feel him relax at her address of him.

"Awwwww." Emily smiled at them. "I've seen a lot of familiars
on the ward, but I've never seen one like him before."

"He is pretty unique," Brigitte agreed. "I'm super lucky he
wanted me as his witch."

I'm luckier. Luckiest.

Emily took back the brush. "You cuddle, and I'll brush while I
tell you what's been going on." She sat behind Brigitte and started
with the tangles at the ends. "Do you know much about demons?"

"I've learned the basics," Brigitte said. "Enough to know
better than to mess with them." Demons were never the best option;
they did their best to twist their caster's word, and even the young
ones were cunning. But they were a common tool of those who

thought they had no other choice.

"Wiser words have never been spoken," Emily agreed. "Anyway, the demon was summoned by a man who'd lost his job about a month ago. His girlfriend took their kid and moved in with her parents. And he'd just gotten an eviction notice."

Brigitte groaned. That was an impressive amount of bad luck all at once. "He didn't make it, did he?" She felt bad it hadn't even occurred to her until that moment.

Emily sighed. "No. I'm afraid not. But the demon's other victims are all stable and expected to recover, for the most part."

"I'm glad to hear that." She didn't want to know about their injuries, or what the qualifier really meant just now.

"That was actually a really high level demon," Emily went on. "You must be crazy strong, because you weren't the first to try to send it back. And if it hadn't been checked, I think a lot of people would have died." She ran the brush down Brigitte's head, and she wondered if this was what it felt like to Hēi Māo when she pet him. "You're a hero."

"Not really," Brigitte said quietly.

"Mrrrrrrr," Hēi Māo disagreed. *Brave. Strong. Best.*

"There's video," Emily said. "You should probably watch it some time, both because you aren't going to be able to avoid it, and because I think it will look different seeing it from where we all did. You really were amazing."

Brigitte shrugged. "I just did what I had to."

Emily moved to the side, continuing to detangle Brigitte's hair. "The person who recorded it, was in a fourth floor apartment, filming from the back. Given the angle, your face is never clear, so no one's been able to identify you yet. And those of us who know, aren't telling." She smiled, giving Brigitte a gentle pat on the shoulder. "Because you had that cloak on, and the way it fluttered and flapped in the wind, people have started calling you Mademoiselle

Butterfly."

"Oh. What happened to my clothes?" Brigitte asked, suddenly realizing she had no memory of being changed and no idea where her things were. She'd been so proud of the capelet, and would be disappointed if it was ruined. Though, now she might not be able to wear it for a while anyway, for fear of being found out.

"Your parents took them home last night, once they were convinced you were all right."

They were back before she woke up, so she hadn't even realized they'd ever been gone. She was glad they hadn't actually slept on the tiny couch.

"Do you know who saved you, though?" Emily asked, her eyebrows arching.

Brigitte bit her lip. She wasn't used to lying, but this wasn't something she was ready to discuss. "Uh, no? I was pretty out of it."

"Well, he looked **just like** Jacque Parenteau, you know, the model? But he's been missing since June." She left that statement there for a moment.

Brigitte swallowed the lump in her throat. "But... um... really?" While she knew the truth in all of that, she and Hēi Māo, or Jacque, rather, hadn't had a chance to discuss any of it. She couldn't out him without permission, and she wasn't sure she would even if he approved. "I... uh, I've been following the news on his disappearance. It sounds, uh, very mysterious. Kind of like how his mother vanished years ago." She now had a whole lot of theories about both of their disappearances.

"Yes, well, this boy fished you out of the river. He did CPR on you, and called for an ambulance on your phone. He saved your life." Emily finished Brigitte's hair and set aside the brush. "Bystanders were able to get closer by the time the paramedics arrived, and they were sure it was Jacque Parenteau, barefoot, with shaggy hair, and wearing jeans that were too short."

"But… is that even possible?" Brigitte asked, rubbing her finger under Hēi Māo's chin.

"He came to the hospital with you, and initially resisted leaving when the doctors wanted to treat you. That part's in your chart." She shook her head slowly. "If it **was** him, and I honestly think it was, it makes me wonder how bad things were for him that he chose to walk away from the life he had."

Brigitte frowned. She'd been so busy wrapping her head around **who** he was that she hadn't really thought too much about **why** he'd been living on the streets. She remembered the shredded bonds, something arcane law was very particular about being applied to another person. She felt like she might cry, given the right nudge. "Are they sure it was him?" she asked, though anyone who'd seen him had to have known. She'd known and she was half drowned.

"That or he has a doppelganger," Emily said. "A couple private investigators showed up at the hospital last night, but we sent them away. They won't hear from us who you are, or that you might know where he is." Her laptop let out a quiet chime. She turned away to open it. "Excellent. You, my dear, are all ready to be discharged. Your parents already got your home care and follow up instructions."

"Home care?" That sounded ominous.

Emily nodded. "It's just the things we recommend you do at home, during your recovery period to help you heal up faster. It's mostly resting, I'm afraid." She tapped a few keys. "Once your parents get here, you're free to go." She held up one finger. "But I want you to take it easy. Go slow. You're going to spend the rest of *les vacances de la Toussaint* convalescing, and you'll probably still miss some school. Right now, your recovery is the most important activity in your life."

Brigitte nodded. "Got it."

Chapter Twenty-One

Hēi Māo practically burrowed into his witch's side for the ride home from the hospital. The family car felt too tiny and crowded, and the tension in the air was like a thick fog, choking him.

Was it possible for a witch to renounce her familiar? If a familiar committed a crime, could they be punished? He'd never heard of such situations, and it terrified him.

Brigitte knew who he was. Of course she did; they were in the same line of business she was pursuing. She was so smart he was honestly a little surprised to have hidden his nature for this long. He should have prepared for this inevitability. He never should have assumed she wouldn't figure him out. Her parents had to know, given what the nurse had said about the video from the fight with the demon. While she was in the hospital, it felt like everything was going to be fine, but now that was a temporary dream of peace, and he was back to fear and panic about their future and if he still had a role in it.

His purr was an anxious plea for forgiveness and a self-soothing act. He had no good excuses for misleading her, though it all felt like the right decision at the time. Yet even if she and her parents hated him now, he could never regret saving her life. He forced himself to focus on that. She was alive. It might not be a bargaining chip, and that was okay, he just needed her safe and healthy.

* * *

Brigitte cuddled her anxiously purring familiar. She wasn't sure how much of the nervous energy in the car was coming from him, how much was her own, and what she was picking up from her parents. It felt like everyone was waiting for something, and she had a pretty good idea what it was.

"I'm sorry for worrying you," she said, leaning her forehead on her window. "I swear, as soon as I felt the prickle of magic, I started straight home."

"We aren't angry, sweetie," her maman said quietly. "It was scary to hear about it. Terrifying to get the call from the hospital, and even more so to see the footage on the news knowing that was you." She twisted in her seat to meet Brigitte's eyes. "But I'm so proud of you. Helping other people in this situation... I'm sure it was frightening for you, too."

Me three.

Brigitte nodded. "Yeah. It was." She sighed. "But it was going after a woman with a pram, and I **had** to do something."

Her mother reached back between the seats and patted her knee.

"When we get home, I think we all need a bit of tea and something sweet," her father suggested. "We'll figure this all out together, Cupcake."

"Your treats are way better than the hospital food," Brigitte insisted.

When they arrived home, she told her parents to go on up ahead, she wanted to make her way on her own since it gave her a bit of time truly alone with her familiar. "We're going to have a family

106

meeting," she explained while she slowly inched her way out of the car. "Tea and sweets are always part of those, just in case it helps with the tough bits."

Hēi Māo looked down at his front paws, seeming sad.

"It's okay, I promise." She gently touched one paw with her fingers. "But we all need to be on the same page."

He scrambled up her arm to her shoulder. *You're mine. I'm yours.*

"Yes," she agreed. "But what do we keep secret and what do we share?" She nuzzled his side with her head. "I'm still your witch. You're still my familiar. And that can't be undone, so it might be a good idea for us to figure out exactly what it means. That's all. " His fur smelled a little like the hospital. "Are you okay? I'm so sorry, I should have asked earlier. Yesterday had to be hard for you, too."

I don't want to think about it.

"Okay." She'd made it in through the side door and started up the steps. "I feel really stupid for naming you Hēi Māo now. I mean, it wasn't even supposed to be your name, but it sort of stuck."

I like it.

"You wouldn't prefer I use your other name?"

You gave it to me. I like it. His words were accompanied by a strong sense of rejection, making it clear how he felt about his old name.

By the time she was lowering herself to the living room chair, her maman had a tea pot brewing, and her papa had brought up a selection of snacks. Hēi Māo moved to Brigitte's lap, leaning against her.

"We're not going to eat you," her father said gently. "But we should meet you properly, Jacque, is it?"

"He doesn't want that name," Brigitte explained, shaking her head.

"Oh," her papa said quietly. "Just how long have you known

your familiar wasn't entirely a cat?"

"Only since yesterday," she said quickly, suddenly worried this wouldn't go as she'd expected. Her parents were sensible and kind, but... they didn't like lies and they could be overprotective at times. "I realized it in the hospital, but... I wasn't entirely with it."

Papa nodded once then turned his gaze back to her familiar. "You had the remnants of magical bindings on you when she found you. Bindings that were probably illegal and that **you'd** broken." He rubbed at his chin. "If they'd been placed by kidnappers, you could have easily returned home once you'd damaged them enough to get away. So you weren't kidnapped, then, were you? You ran away. But the bonds..." A look of disgust crossed his face. "Were those placed by your family?"

Do you hate me? His voice was so small in her head.

"Of course we don't hate you," Brigitte said, quite sharply. "You're part of our family now, no matter where you came from or how you joined us."

Her father nodded. "She's right, Hēi Māo. Be a good lad and let us see you... hmmm not as you truly are, because you're as much cat as anything. But let us see your other form."

With a sigh, Hēi Māo dropped to the floor. There was a flash of green light, and the black cat was gone. In his place crouched a sixteen-year-old boy with shaggy blond hair, ill fitting clothes, and spectacular green eyes.

Brigitte reached down to the boy crouched by her feet. He was nervous, afraid, even. She could feel it just like she could when he was a cat. "I know you," she said, smiling as she rested a hand on his shoulder. She'd always reassured him with physical touch, so she tried that first. "You really **did** fish me out of the river."

He nodded and sat back, leaning on her chair, with one arm around her legs.

"Aah," her papa said, smiling. "Now your aura is human, but

slightly odd. So you are truly both cat **and** boy."

"You're a shape-shifter," her maman said, delighted. "I've met so few shape-shifters in France."

"You might've met more without knowing," Brigitte said, thinking back to her first history lesson with him.

"We don't really advertise what we are," the boy said quietly. It was Hēi Māo's voice, the one she heard sometimes at night and when he rescued her from bad dreams. Brigitte could see the magic of her collar around his neck even though the collar itself had vanished with his transformation. "A lot of people don't trust us, which is ridiculous, because other magic users can mask and change their appearance, too. I can't masquerade as someone else. I just become a cat."

"Is your family all shape-shifters?" her maman asked.

He shook his head. "My father has a little witchcraft, but my maman was a shape-shifter." He hesitated a moment. "Father didn't know about either of us until I shifted in front of him in my crib." He shrugged. "At that point it was pretty obvious, so she came clean." He rested his chin on Brigitte's knees. "I'm not sure he ever trusted her after he found out. And he's never trusted me." He froze and curled in on himself.

"What's wrong?" Brigitte asked, suddenly picking up his fear and sadness.

"I've betrayed you all," he whispered. "I've only given you reasons to mistrust me."

"When you're fleeing for your life, some lying might be necessary," Maman said, understanding quicker than Brigitte expected. "I do ask you to not continue the habit now that your secrets are out. We can't help you if you keep us in the dark. And we can't trust you, if you won't trust us."

"Trust goes both ways, son," Papa added. "I'm hoping you can learn to trust us as we get to know each other better. And Ling is right. You had good reasons before. You couldn't be sure how we would react."

"What made you run away?" Maman asked.

"My whole life was this isolated, structured nightmare, a polar opposite to my nature." He swallowed. "Before my maman vanished, we used to shift when my father was at work or away at conferences. If he brought us on his trips, it was how we spent our days in our hotel room." He shuddered. "When she disappeared, he got even more strict. I was almost always supervised. And he didn't want me shifting at all."

"That's horrible," Brigitte blurted, getting more furious with each new detail.

He nodded, his eyes on her feet. "If I don't shift once a week I start to get jittery and itchy. But he didn't care. He..." He faltered on his own words. "He found some magical restraints that were crafted to prevent shifting."

When she noticed he was unconsciously rubbing his wrists, she gently caught his hand, raising it to look more closely. She could see hints of residual magic on his skin, and she frowned. "I'll take care of these tonight."

His head shot up and he met her eyes. "No. You need to rest. It can wait." He shook his head. "I can wait." He looked at her parents again. "The only time I was allowed out of my room was for modeling. He told me we were stuck with each other, but at least I was handsome enough to make up for some of my flaws. When the opportunity came up in June, I ran away."

"I'm so sorry to hear all this," her maman said, reaching forward, then hesitating. "I'd like to hug you, Hēi Māo, but you're still a familiar and... goodness this is strange."

"Would you like a hug?" Brigitte asked him. "I'm okay with my parents touching you if you're comfortable with it."

His nod was quick and jerky, like he felt he had to answer

before she could change her mind.

Maman dropped to her knees and wrapped her arms around him. "Whatever happened before, you're our family now," she promised. He pressed his forehead to her shoulder, breathing in erratic audible gasps.

"I'm so sorry," he whined. "He's going to try to get me back. I know he will. He doesn't want this horrible family secret to get out."

"You're my familiar," Brigitte said gently, resting her hand on the back of his head. "No one can break a familiar contract, and the law is on our side here."

He turned to look up at her, his eyes wet. "I know. And I feel terrible because while it keeps me safe from him, it doesn't protect you and your family from everything he can do." He gulped. "My father is a really awful person."

"I take down demons in my free time, Kitty," Brigitte said simply. "I'm not scared of your father."

He hiccuped and giggled, sounding a little hysterical. "You're amazing, you know that?"

* * *

"You said you were going to stay a cat, but didn't plan to become a familiar," Ling said. "What changed your mind?"

"I'd always been told to watch out for witches, to stay away from them. My father said I'd get stolen or worse," he explained, desperate for them to understand. He'd been fully willing to give up comfort, even his humanity, to get away from his father. He hoped Brigitte could feel his sincerity through their familiar bond despite his change in form. He could feel her distress and worry, so it seemed both likely and hopeful. "But then I saw you, walking the streets in the late afternoon, talking to the strays and obviously looking for the right one." He settled his chin on her knee again and looked up at her. He felt her surprise, and something sweeter, a sense of appreciation and delight, like she felt honored that he'd chosen her, and that was definitely a promising reaction. "I saw how you were. No net. No ropes. No catnip. You wanted the cats to come to you. You were patient. You waited. You spoke to them." He smiled.

"I find it concerning that you would choose the path of a familiar, binding yourself to someone permanently." Although not stern, Nik's voice had gone serious. "Did you understand what you were agreeing to?"

Hēi Māo nodded. "I knew enough, more than most cats do."

"Most cats don't make a conscious choice," Nik pointed out. "You knew what Brigitte was doing when you found her. You encouraged her to keep you."

"I did," Hēi Māo agreed. "I'd already decided to stay a cat for the rest of my life. Being a familiar would mean I wouldn't ever have to go back to my father."

"Safe," Brigitte said, straightening up. "That's what you said after our ceremony. You chose to be my familiar because you'd be safe."

"That was only part of it," he said quickly. "I've never liked being alone, and I wanted to help you. I thought maybe I could do it, that maybe it was what I was meant for." He reached out and gently touched her nose with one finger. "When you brought me home, it all felt right. It was like I belonged here. And you respected cat-me more than my father respected **any** version of me." He looked down at her feet again.

"You know it's a bond you can't walk away from, right?" Nik asked.

Hēi Māo's arm wrapped tighter around her legs. "I would never!" he said, indignant. "That part I understood, and it's a commitment I take very seriously." He gazed up at Brigitte, desperate. "It's the little things I didn't understand. I knew I'd have a role in your magic, in helping you. And I want to do that. You've been so good to me. I'm just sorry I wasn't entirely honest from the start."

She ran her hand over his head. "I understand, and I forgive you."

He relaxed, pressing his face to her knee for a moment.

"When did you first see her?" Nik asked.

Hēi Māo took a deep breath as he thought. "Eight or nine days before I convinced her to take me home." He sat up, loosening his hold on his witch. They hadn't yelled at him yet. Their tone and body language, Brigitte's words on the way up, all assured him that maybe this would be okay.

"Really?" Brigitte demanded. "How? I never noticed you."

He smiled slyly. "I'm a black cat. I'm clever."

"And you weren't already looking for a witch at that point?" Nik asked.

Hēi Māo shook his head. "At first I didn't really think much of it, other than making sure to hide." He turned so he could appeal directly to his witch. "But after watching her with the other strays, I couldn't stop thinking about her. And a familiar I'd met made me look at things differently." He sighed. "I'm sorry. I've made such a mess for you."

"No, Hēi Māo," Nik said gently. "Your father may have made a mess of you, but I don't think any of us regret having you here."

He stared at Nik in shock. How could they be so understanding? His own father didn't love him half this much.

"We're going to have to rethink a few things," Nik went on. "But I know we can make this work for all of us."

"Now that this is out in the open," Ling said. "Nik and I have some business we need to attend to." She got to her feet. "Brigitte, I want you to do a little online shopping with Hēi Māo to see that he has clothes that fit. I'll text you a budget once I've had a chance to consider finances. And Hēi Māo, I need you to make sure she rests.

It would help us with our tasks."

Her hug earlier had been so warm and loving, and now she was entrusting him with her daughter's well-being? This was all so far beyond his wildest dreams when he dared to consider coming clean to his witch; he wasn't sure how to react beyond quiet obedience.

"What are you going to do, Maman?" Brigitte asked, as she slowly stood.

"We'll explain at dinner," Nik answered. "It's not your concern, either of your concern for now. We should have something more useful to share once you've rested a bit."

"Come on Kitty." Brigitte tugged gently at his hand. "Let's get you some clothes." He followed her up to the room that had grown so comfortable in the last few weeks.

Chapter Twenty-Two

While it was definitely strange to be leading her familiar to her room in the form of a boy, it also felt normal. It was like some part of her brain had known what he was all along, or that she'd put together some of the pieces that made him so odd as a cat, and it just all made sense now.

Her eyes caught the cat tree as she headed to her desk chair. "I think I need to ask you about a few things, but... it's going to be awkward."

He took the chair next to her and bent to gently rub his cheek on her shoulder. "**You** can ask me anything." He straightened up and turned those beautiful green eyes on her. "I can feel you're worried, but I know anything you ask will come from a place of respect, even if it comes out wrong."

She nodded, trying to find the right starting point. "Have I ever made you uncomfortable?"

He shook his head, looking a little surprised.

"So the way I treat you in your cat form... that's been all right? It's not demeaning or anything?"

He beamed at her and it was like the room was suddenly

filled with sunshine. "I love how you treat cat-me. Please don't change a thing."

That was a relief. She'd been caught by the sudden thought that she'd been pedantic and rude. "And how do you like to be treated when you're a person?"

He stared at her, eyes wide for a moment, as though desperately trying to find an answer to her question. "I have no idea," he finally admitted. "My father treated me like a burden and an asset. I think other models and photographers only saw me as a potential path to someone who could influence their careers." His fingers drummed nervously on her desktop. "It's been so long, I barely remember what it was like to have someone who genuinely liked me and didn't try to control who or what I was. I don't really know who I am, who I want to be."

Brigitte felt a little pain in her chest that had nothing to do with her injuries. Before he could downplay his statement, she took his nearer hand in both of hers, effectively stilling him. "I want you to be yourself, whoever that is." Though her voice was gentle, it held no flexibility. "And I'm going to be here for you as you try to figure that out, okay?"

He nodded, and she could feel his surprise. "Thank you," he whispered reverently. After a moment he looked up again. "I didn't think of it before, but... have I made you uncomfortable? Are there things I need to do differently?"

Realizing she'd been sharing her room with a teenage boy was a little awkward, but when she thought about everything he'd done, she couldn't fault his actions. "I think you've done pretty well, actually. But some things are going to take a little getting used to, like your cat behaviors in human form." She didn't dislike those, exactly, but they were a bit weird.

"Should I... not do those?" His eyebrows furrowed in thought.

She shook her head, then shrugged. "I'm not sure you even

realize you're doing it, and it's not like it's awful or embarrassing. It's more unexpected."

He nodded. "You can always tell me if something's not okay, too."

"Yeah. Talking about this kind of thing is going to be important for us." Their relationship, complicated though it had become, was a critical component of both of their futures. They'd have to be really careful to avoid miscommunication. "What do you want me to call you when you're in you human guise?" Based on their earlier conversation she had a strong suspicion, but she needed to be sure.

"I like being Hēi Māo," he said, smiling happily. "And I'm still me, no matter which form I wear."

She nodded. "I know. But I think people will be confused when you're out and about in human form and I call you that."

He stared at her, nearly stunned to speechlessness. "I'll be **allowed** to go out in my human form?" His voice was a whisper.

"Did you really think we'd make you stay a cat in public?" The fact that, that had been his first assumption made her feel near tears again. "I want you to feel free to take whichever form you want." She could feel the arcane support and boost to her strength she'd gotten from him since their bonding, even when she wasn't actively casting. She wrinkled her face a bit. "You're still my familiar, either way, and I don't think this is something we're going to be able to keep secret, no matter how hard we try. Besides, I don't want to try. I want you to be you."

He nodded, overwhelmed. "I like it when you call me Kitty," he said shyly. "It reminds me that I'm **your** kitty. But in a sweet way. Not like you own me."

She laughed. "Technically, we own each other." He probably didn't understand all the nuances of their contract. She'd have to help him with that.

He nodded. "Are your parents going to be okay with me going out in public..." She felt his realization, though she couldn't see what it was. "**That's** why your maman wanted you to get me clothes?" he asked eagerly. "So I can be a guy sometimes, too?"

She nodded, reaching out to nudge his hair out of his face. Like a cat, he leaned into her hand, rubbing his cheek against her palm. Leaning away for a moment, she opened a drawer and took out a tape measure. "You've grown since you got those clothes. May I measure you so we can get the right sizes?"

He nodded and stood up, pulling his shirt over his head in a smooth movement. Before she could stop him, he'd dropped his jeans to the floor and was pushing them away with one foot.

"Uhh. You didn't have to strip," she said, feeling the heat in her cheeks.

"**Really**?" he sounded surprised. "This is how they always take my measurements at work."

For the first time, it fully connected in her brain that actual teen model and heartthrob Jacque Parenteau was her familiar. He was **her** kitty, and he was standing in front of her in his underwear.

"Did I embarrass you?" he asked, wrapping his arms around himself as if they would hide his thin form.

She waved off his concern. "You're a model and a cat. Of course you have no modesty whatsoever." She smiled at him. "Let me pull up my worksheet." She'd developed a spreadsheet for measurements, with the ones she needed most often highlighted. Moving slowly, she wrapped the flexible fabric measure around his waist. "And what does my kitty like to do?" she asked. "Do you have any hobbies or interests?" Checking the number she turned toward her computer and entered it. She had to move slowly, pivoting the chair because twisting her body was just too uncomfortable.

"I like video games and anime," he said. Holding his arms straight out to the side and out of her way as she captured his hip and chest measurements. "I read a lot." He paused in thought. "I used to take piano, fencing and Mandarin lessons."

She was reminded of his first act of help. "Thanks again for the flash cards. They're the best."

He smiled down at her where she was measuring his shoulder to wrist. "I've always found flashcards helpful."

She handed him the end of the tape. "I need your in and out-seam. Can you hold that end?"

He held it exactly where he needed to, demonstrating his experience with the process. "You're really smart, and I like studying with you."

She glanced at him over her shoulder as she entered the latest numbers. "I'm glad. But we'll have to change that up a bit. You should get to learn, too."

"I **do**," he said happily. "I **like** going to school with you."

"I knew you were always paying attention." She'd been suspicious of that, even when she thought he was just a cat. "You like physics, I can tell."

He laughed and picked up his pants as she put away the measuring tape. "Physics comes naturally, but my favorite is probably math, maybe statistics and probability.

"What do you want to look at first, shirts, pants, socks... you need everything." She opened her browser.

"You pick." He settled in the chair while he inverted his shirt. "I've never done this before."

She realized then that while his clothes were a little ratty and small, they were designer. Like everything he'd probably ever worn. "Have you ever gotten to pick out your own clothes?"

"For buying, no." He shook his head. "My father's assistant always brought me my new clothes and took away anything I'd outgrown."

Brigitte scowled at her computer screen as she pulled up a

clothing store Ruhul liked. "**You** get to pick what we're buying, though we'll have a spending limit, so we need to be reasonable," she explained. "And once I'm feeling better, I'd like to make you some clothes designed just for you, with colors, fabrics, and designs you pick, okay?"

"You'd want to do that for me?" his voice was so small and surprised.

"Of course I would," she assured him. She'd have to talk to her parents about giving him the opportunity to make choices whenever possible, even if it was simple things like planning dinner or picking a movie.

After they had ordered several t-shirts and some jeans, he was nonchalantly scrolling through underwear. It was a little disconcerting that he kept asking her opinion on color and design, until she reminded herself that she and Aalia did the same thing.

"What was it like, living as a stray cat?" she asked. She already knew about his father, but felt she should find out if there was any other trauma he might need help managing.

He shrugged, adding something to the cart and turning to look at her. "At first, it was really nice. I felt free for the first time in my life, and it was... that was wonderful. Honestly, that part never got old." He sighed. "But I couldn't find a cat colony where I fit. They could all tell I wasn't just a cat, and they thought I'd bring trouble. So I was mostly alone, and that wasn't really any different than living with my father."

There was the isolation again. They'd have to work on that. "Where did you live?" He really was clever, given he'd managed to live on the streets for five months without getting hurt or caught. Stray males could be territorial and aggressive, but he'd either won those fights without injury, or he'd avoided them. She wasn't quite ready to ask about that.

"I moved around a lot. I had to, to keep my father from finding me." Leaning his elbows on the desk, he rested his chin on one fist. "There was this one acupuncture parlor where the owner was really nice. If I came by at the right time, he'd feed me canned salmon and he talked to me a lot." He hesitated. "I think he might have known what I was, but it didn't bother him. He called me Tom, and showed me a sheltered spot where his furnace vented. It was a nice place to sleep when it was cold at night."

"Do you remember where it was?" Brigitte asked.

He nodded. "It's not far from here." He straightened up and reached for the mouse again. "Why?"

She was pretty sure he was talking about Master Fu's place. It reinforced her theory that Hēi Māo was the black tom whose chi matched hers. "I want to thank him for taking care of my kitty."

Hēi Māo turned to her, his vibrant eyes wide. She felt a rush of affection and gratefulness from him, things that were apparently beyond words, because he quickly looked down without speaking.

"I want you to be happy," she said quietly, resting a gentle hand on his shoulder. "You're such a wonderful person... er being?"

He smiled. "Either works. Or cat, too."

She nodded. "You've made me happy. You've been so sweet and kind. You bring me flowers and breakfast..." she hesitated. "How **did** you get me flowers, you clever kitty?"

"Oh!" He stood up abruptly. "Stay here." He scurried up to her bed, pushed open the skylight and went out on the terrace.

She marveled at how fluid his movements were, like a cat in human form. It was no wonder he was a natural on the runway.

His footsteps were light on the roof, and after a few moments, he returned with a tattered black backpack. He set it down between his bare feet and unzipped it. "This is what I had with me when I ran away. He pulled out a jacket, some rope, a notepad, and a plastic bag holding a wallet, and a pile of euro notes. "The first thing I did was withdraw some money. It was going to be my safety net in case it got too cold at night and I needed a place to stay, or if I just couldn't hack it as a cat."

It looked like a lot of money, actually. "Did you need to use it much?"

He shook his head. "I'm a pretty good hunter... uh... maybe we won't talk about what I ate, though. Not sure you'd appreciate it." His pale cheeks flushed.

"Are you telling me you ate like a cat?" she asked, feigning shock. "How... biologically appropriate of you."

He laughed. "Okay. Thanks. But I promise not to gift you with any mice or birds."

"Oh thank **god**." She didn't even try to hide her relief. "If you must get me something, the flowers or the breakfast are just fine."

He grinned. "Noted."

Chapter Twenty Three

She yawned, and the weariness she'd been subduing while she ordered him new clothes, was suddenly apparent in her posture.

"You need to rest," he said, frowning a little. He should have made her do it sooner, but he was having too much fun getting to know her better. He stood up and looked around her room. "I don't think you should be up in the loft until you can get up and down by yourself." He pulled at his lip with two fingers, puzzling over the best way to make her comfortable enough to sleep. The nurse had been quite insistent that recovering needed to be her primary focus. Her bed was comfortable, but he didn't want her on the ladder. "Is it okay if I bring down your mattress?"

She shrugged. "If you want."

Leaving her settled on her chaise, he climbed up to push her pillows and blankets down. There was something oddly satisfying in shoving them over the guard rail. It was probably the cat in him. The mattress took a bit more work, since he didn't want it to hit anything, but before long, he'd relocated her entire bed to the floor.

He pulled back the blankets and patted the mattress. "Come

on Brigitte. It's nap time."

"What are you going to do?" she asked, wincing as she lay down.

"I'm going to watch over you," he promised. "Do you prefer a cat guard or a person."

"Whichever you want," she insisted.

"And is it still okay if I'm on your bed?" he asked. That was a whole special can of worms he hadn't even realized needed opening until now. She'd technically been sharing her bed with a cat and a teenage guy. Even with his sheltered upbringing, he knew that was creepy, and he felt terrible for not realizing it until now. Maybe it would be best to sleep as a cat from now on. He could do that if it made things less awkward.

"You're my familiar **and** a cat," she pointed out, smiling as she closed her eyes. "You can go wherever you want."

He sat down beside her, watching her face and monitoring his arcane awareness of her emotions for any hint of discomfort. He was still shaken by yesterday's accident, by her dance with death. But his need to be near her wasn't more important than her comfort. He was relieved to feel that she was soothed by his presence. Smiling to himself, he slowly reached out, gently resting his hand on her hair. He whispered, "I'll be right here if you need me."

* * *

Brigitte woke achy and warm to the hushed whispers of her mother and her familiar. "Kih-ee," she mumbled, reaching behind herself, only to feel cold blankets.

"But what if... " Hēi Māo was upset, bordering on terrified. The echo of his panic was probably what woke her up.

"You're not going anywhere," her maman replied firmly. "Nik consulted a lawyer friend of ours. She's agreed to act on our behalf, even if it's just for a formal agreement."

"He'll target your business," he warned. "I've… he's done it before. For lesser… offenses."

"Which is why we'll go for a legal contract to prevent the ugliness," her mother said, in her most soothing voice. But it wasn't enough.

"Hēi Māo?" Brigitte blinked, her eyes feeling gooey and stuck. She sat up, gasping at the sharp pain in her ribs. "Ah!" There were suddenly warm bodies on either side of her, gently holding her up.

"Didn't the nurse explain how you should get up?" her mother asked, a hint of reprimand in her voice. "Roll to the side and push yourself up with your arms."

Brigitte nodded, wincing and trying to force her gasps to be shallow. "Yeah," she mumbled. "She said something about Cleopatra rising from her barge," she huffed. "Like we have any idea how Cleopatra actually got up."

"She was talking about golden age film Cleopatra, Brigitte." Hēi Māo rubbed her cheek with his. "But next time let me help."

She nodded, then focused carefully on him. He was still worried about something. She looked at her mother. "Did Papa really talk to a lawyer?" It didn't surprise her that he already had a plan, it was his way, but she **was** surprised how fast he moved.

Her mother nodded. "Yes. And it's a good thing, too." She sighed. "Monsieur Parenteau has been alerted to the fact that his son saved Mademoiselle Butterfly. That's what they're calling you, you know." She rubbed Brigitte's back. "He's pestering the police to release your information to him so he and his own private investigator can personally question you."

Brigitte gawked at her mother. The demand was both frightening and wildly inappropriate.

"As both cases are under police jurisdiction and you're a minor, they aren't willing to cooperate, but as Hēi Māo said, his father can be quite difficult." She gave Brigitte one last squeeze before standing up. "The detective you talked to after the incident with Celeste is going to stop in tomorrow. We've agreed to talk with him, because the police can help us if they know what's going on. Fortunately he was understanding that we have far too much on our plate for today, so he'll be by in the morning. He also seems sympathetic to you, Brigitte, so it would be good for you to meet with him as well."

Brigitte felt Hēi Māo's tension rise and leaned against him a little more. "Are you okay?"

He nodded, a jerky snap of his head.

"I need you two to think about how you want to handle this," her mother explained. "If Hēi Māo wants to go out in human form, which is only fair, but you should be prepared to release a statement."

Feeling foggy and stupid, Brigitte stared at her mother. "Why?"

"I think it'll be easy for people to figure out you're Mademoiselle Butterfly if they see us together," Hēi Māo said quietly. "And it probably won't be long before someone notices that I'm your familiar. And based on the previous video, it'll be obvious I'm a shape-shifter." He sighed. "Would it be easier if I stay in cat form outside of home?" he asked. "I was prepared to live out my life as a cat anyway, so..."

"No!" Brigitte cried.

At the very same time her mother let out a sharp, **"Absolutely not!"** Smiling proudly at Brigitte, she continued. "We aren't going to restrict you, Hēi Māo. Since you're Brigitte's familiar, she would be within her rights, by ancient arcane law, to do so. But **we** are modern witches, and you are not **just** her familiar or **just** a cat. It would be unforgivable for us to violate your basic human rights as your father did." Her hand reached out and hovered over his head for a moment.

Hēi Māo's eyes met Brigitte's briefly, as if confirming he had permission, before pushing his crown against her mother's palm.

"Oh, you sweet boy," she said, sadness creeping into her voice. "You deserve a good life, an education of your choosing, and friends. You may be bound to our daughter for the rest of your lives, but that isn't all there is to you. Not by a long shot." Her hand ran over his head. "And we are prepared to do what we need to, to help you get that life."

Brigitte felt a vibration from him and she grinned. "You're purring!"

Blushing, he ducked his head. "I've been cat so much lately, that part of my nature is... a little more at the fore than normal."

I like it, Brigitte thought, wondering if he could pick up her mental speech in this form.

His small, almost secretive smile told her he could.

Her mother took a step back. "You two have a talk. Decide what you want to volunteer to the detective, and what you want to withhold. I don't think you should lie, but I also don't expect he'll push too much if there's anything you don't want to talk about." She headed for the stairs. "I'll send Callie up when it's dinner time."

Chapter Twenty-Four

Hēi Māo was in his human form. While he still felt like himself, something subtle was off. He fidgeted as he tried to puzzle through it, only able to identify it as something arcane. It was dark, and for some reason he couldn't see as well as normal. A cat had excellent night vision, and as a human, a cat shape-shifter had far better than average night vision. He **should** be able to see better than this. Where was he that it could possibly be so very dark?

Shifting cost him nothing. When he was little, and still learning to control it, the necessary focus was exhausting, but in a mental way. He remembered napping in his mother's lap after switching back and forth dozens of times in an hour. The routine morning exercises had gone on for two years until he'd fully mastered his control. He closed his eyes and basked in the warm glow of those days for a moment. The obstacle courses she'd set up for him, then timed him running through had been just challenging enough to be fun. The touch of his mother's hand on his head, in either form, as he snuggled with her afterward. He felt his purr vibrate in his chest as he relaxed with the memory.

Opening his eyes again, he was determined to figure this out.

He patted the space around him, pulling at the blankets of the bed he sat on. The sheets were lovely and soft, nicer than Brigitte's. He froze for a moment before moving to his hands and knees, patting the bed and sniffing the air. She wasn't here. She wasn't with him. This wasn't her bed.

Fully panicked now, he shifted. Or intended to. But nothing happened. He tried again, paying close attention to how the magic gathered before dissipating into his wrists. He grasped his wrists, whimpering when he found the hated arcane manacles his father used to restrict his shifting. His father had been worried about him randomly shifting when he was excited, despite years of evidence that it wouldn't be a problem. Bracelets, the man had called them, but that was just a front.

Tipping onto his side and curling into a ball, he heard himself whine. No no no. This couldn't be happening. He was safe now, with his witch. She was his home. She wouldn't let this happen to him.

It's okay, she whispered. I'm right here.

The comforting touch of her mind against his left him boneless and weeping in a heap. Where was she? How had this happened?

It's a nightmare, Kitty, she explained. I'm with you right now. I would never let anything happen to you.

He knew that. He really did. But a traitorous part of his brain reminded him that even a powerful witch couldn't prevent everything. For a moment he thought he could feel the phantom touch of her hand in his hair.

Come back to me, Kitty, she said. Wake up and come back.

He shook himself a little, or maybe that was her. And when he opened his eyes this time, he found himself in the pink room he loved. Brigitte was sitting up on the mattress they shared, leaning over him as much as she could with her sore ribs, her hand buried in his hair. His face was wet and hot.

He sat up, wanting nothing more than to clamber in her lap, but that would hurt her. He wasn't even sure how she'd sat up.

"It's okay, Kitty," she whispered out loud this time. Both her thumbs came up to sweep away his tears. "We're both safe. We're both home."

"I couldn't shift," he blurted, his mind still clinging to that horror.

She frowned. "I'm so sorry. You've been through such awful things, and it's not fair."

He followed her gentle nudges, allowing her to gather him close for a hug. It was instantly soothing.

"I won't ever let that happen again, okay?" Her hand was in his hair. "Your father has no legal standing on the issue, as he'll find out when we meet in a few days. Even if he did, I would never let him take you back. You'll never wear those awful manacles again." Her hands moved to pat his wrists. "And if anyone tries to take you..." He felt her take a deep breath, steadying her voice as it had gone wobbly. "A witch can always find her familiar. I **will** come for you."

Her reasoning came as a relief, but he still worried. She'd never met his father.

She lifted his head, wincing a little. "You've boosted my power far beyond a normal familiar. Anyone who thinks they can come between us, will regret it in a very brutal fashion."

He smiled, the safe warmth returning to him at last. He nodded. *Thank you.* He patted her pillows. "Now lie down. You need to rest."

"Only if you rest with me."

"Yes, my Brigitte." He eased her back onto her pillows before snuggling up beside her.

"It's my turn to keep you safe," she whispered, settling a

hand on his shoulder.

* * *

It was wonderful to be able to fetch his Brigitte's breakfast entirely on his own, gathering up something more hearty than a bun with jam. It felt so good to be able to switch from cat to human whenever he wanted. He was arranging things on the her tray when her mama walked in.

"*Zǎo shang hǎo, māma*," he greeted, wishing her a good morning. He liked that he could call her mama instead of Ling now.

She beamed at him. Even when he was still just a cat as far as she knew, she'd been delighted with his apparent understanding of her first language. "*Zǎo shang hǎo wǒ nǚ ér de dà māo.*"

He was amused that she referred to him as her daughter's big cat.

She lightly patted his back, a touch that felt warm and comforting. Brigitte had given her parents permission to touch him if he was okay with it, and they'd decided it felt less of a violation when he was in his human form. "Bringing my daughter her breakfast, are you?"

He nodded, eagerly. "She didn't sleep as well as she could have, and she still has a lot of healing to do."

Mama frowned a little. "Is she okay?"

He nodded, ducking into the cupboard for a glass to hide his blush. "I... I accidentally woke her up," he admitted. "I have bad dreams sometimes... not as many since coming here." He watched his fingers as he poured the milk, not sure he could stand it if he'd disappointed his new mama.

"Oh, sweetie, I'm sorry." She sounded so sincere, he couldn't help looking up, finding sadness and sympathy he still wasn't used to.

He shrugged. "It's not as often now," he pointed out, hoping to ease her mind. She fretted much the way his own maman had. "I feel safe here. I think the familiar bond keeps a lot of that away."

She nodded. "I suppose it would." She gently caught one of his hands as he set a glass of juice on the tray. Turning his palm up, she lightly traced the line around his wrist that only those with the sight could see, an arcane scar from years of wearing shift-blocking bracelets. "I know Brigitte wants to tend to these herself, but Nik or I would be willing to do it if she's not up for it. Please talk to her about it," she requested. "I think getting rid of the magical vestiges of your... imprisonment, will help."

"I'll ask," he promised, knowing that he'd also let his Brigitte know he'd rather wait until she was ready. He liked her parents and even trusted them, but this felt like something he wanted from her. His experiences with magic had been so bad for so long, he really preferred to only be touched by his witch's.

"There's one last thing I want you to discuss with my daughter and your witch," she said, gently squeezing his hand before letting go. "I've done some looking, and I've found a therapist who specializes in magical trauma in younger people."

He nodded, it was a good idea. "Yes," he agreed. "Brigitte should see them."

Mama smiled, letting out a huff of air. "Well, yes, Brigitte should see her. But so should you." She shook her head. "Nik and I are serious, Hēi Māo. We want you to be as healthy and as happy as you can be, and not just because you are bound to our daughter. You deserve it."

"Oh." Joy was a warm fuzzy feeling, something he was still getting used to.

"What you've been through isn't right, and I worry." She added a napkin to the tray. "I think it would be good for both of you to see Dr. Wheeler for a bit. It can be together or on your own. And she may have ideas for helping you deal with those nightmares. I know they are less frequent, but they need to stop entirely."

He nodded. It was a good idea. He'd immediately agreed when he thought it was for the benefit of his Brigitte, but he realized it applied to himself as well. He was still trying to grasp that the way his father had treated him was actually abusive. It was a huge mental shift from the more tolerant idea that his father had been merely strict and controlling. On some level, he knew Brigitte was right, but it was hard to accept that he'd lived it and not realized how bad it was.

He picked up the tray and carefully returned to his witch's side. She was just starting to stir, shoving blankets aside as she usually did before waking up. *Are you hungry?* he asked. Speaking mind to mind was a much gentler wake up.

"Hmmm," she started to stretch, flinching with a wince as she moved unwisely.

"Careful, Brigitte," he cautioned, crawling over the mattress to her. "I'll help you up." He cupped her shoulders to ease her up without putting strain on her ribcage.

"I don't have to be Cleopatra today?" she asked, smirking at him.

He shook his head, smiling. "Not if I'm here." He immediately moved to pile pillows behind her. "You helped me last night, and now it's my turn... if you'll let me."

Chapter Twenty-Five

Brigitte walked slowly down the stairs, leaning heavily on Hēi Māo's arm. There was a definite bonus to her familiar being able to assume a human shape; he was able to help her much more than he could as a cat. She kept her head up, watching the detective as she moved into the family room. His eyes were wide, and she could practically see steam coming out of his ears as he worked through the logistics of Jacque Parenteau being here and this closely acquainted with her. She waited to greet him until she sat down, so she wouldn't get quite so out of breath.

"Good evening, Detective DuValle," she said, offering up a smile. She and Hēi Māo had come to what she felt was a pretty good plan. "I'm sorry to keep you waiting."

"How badly were you hurt?" he asked in surprise.

Hēi Māo whimpered and tucked his head under her chin.

She ran her fingers into his hair and whispered to him. "It's okay, Kitty. You saved me, remember?" She looked back up, seeing confusion on the detective's face. "Technically, I drowned. CPR saved my life, but it also left me really sore."

Detective DuValle nodded. "Aah, yes. I saw the video." He

cleared his throat. "It wasn't comfortable to watch."

Brigitte nodded. "I haven't seen it yet, but that's what I've heard." She gently nudged Hēi Māo out from her neck, finding it a bit strange that it still felt natural when he was in this form. "I understand you have questions, and we want to help you with that, but the situation is complicated."

The detective nodded. "I see that." He sighed and held out his hand to Hēi Māo. "We haven't met. I'm Detective DuValle. I've worked with Brigitte before and–" He jerked his hand back before Hēi Māo could respond. "Oh hell."

"Does that mean you see his collar or that you realize what he is?" Brigitte asked quietly.

"Both." He rubbed at his face. "Jacque Parenteau is your familiar."

Brigitte wrapped her arm around Hēi Māo's when he tensed at the name.

"He was here last time I saw you, as your cat," the detective continued. "So either he was abducted and ensorceled, or he's a shape-shifter and he ran away from home."

Brigitte nodded. "Care to guess which of those is the correct story?"

He let out another sigh, slouching a bit. "You ran away from that man, didn't you?"

Hēi Māo nodded.

"When she brought you home to become her familiar, did you know what she had in mind, what it meant for you?" he asked.

Hēi Māo nodded again. "I... I asked her to take me home. I wanted to be her familiar."

"Did you really know what it meant, what you were signing up for?" the detective asked.

"Mostly." Hēi Māo nodded. "We make each other stronger. And it's permanent."

"And did you tell her what you were?" the detective pressed, both eyebrows raised.

Hēi Māo shook his head. "I'd planned to stay a cat. She wasn't supposed to find out." He looked down at his bare toes. "But there was that demon, and..." He faltered, shrugging. "You know."

Detective DuValle stared at her familiar for a moment. "You deceived her. You realize that, don't you?" His voice was firm, but less hostile than the words hinted at. "Do you understand that you went about it in a way that was unfair to her?"

"Yes." Hēi Māo's voice was small. "We've... we discussed it. I know it was wrong, and I'm grateful that she, and her family, have forgiven me."

The detective nodded once. "Very good." He pulled out a small tablet and started swiping his fingers across it. "All right. I can close your missing person case, Jacque..." He stopped when Hēi Māo flinched again.

"Could you please call him Hēi Māo?" Brigitte asked. "Or maybe... Tom?" She glanced at him, waiting for his response.

Yes.

She nodded. "Hēi Māo or Tom, please. He doesn't want the other name anymore."

Detective DuValle let out a harsh breath, something in his face horrified.

"Are you okay, detective?" Brigitte asked. Between his dressing down of her familiar and this, she hoped they weren't getting a peek at prejudice.

He held up one finger as if requesting a moment to compose himself. He cleared his throat before speaking again. "I have a daughter your age, I believe she's in your class, Brigitte."

She nodded.

"I can't imagine what I'd have to do to make her not want her name anymore." He blinked a little more rapidly than normal, then addressed Hēi Māo again. "In case you aren't ready to talk about it, I'm not going to ask, but if there's anything you need to tell me about why you ran away, my door is always open. Brigitte has my card."

Brigitte smiled at him. "Thank you, detective."

He nodded sharply. "Now, Tom, then, I can let your... father... know you've been found, that you're safe, but that I can't release your location at this time. You are probably going to need to meet with him at some point to get him to back off."

Brigitte looked over to the kitchen, where her mother was watching the proceedings. They shared a silent nod. "My parents are working on that."

Chapter Twenty-Six

Hēi Māo stared at the crepes and berry sauce on his plate, suddenly unsure if he could eat without throwing up. While he'd known they couldn't put off his father's insistent inquiries forever, he'd hoped to be more settled in his new relationship with his witch and her family, with them knowing him and his history, before exposing them to that ugliness. He wasn't ready to face the man who manacled his magic and then hunted him in the streets of Paris like a game animal.

Mama and Papa continued to talk as they performed their usual morning dance in the kitchen, moving around each other as though choreographed or magicked to keep them from colliding. His witch spoke up now and again, but he no longer heard words. The sounds blurred together and he slouched, retreating into himself. Maybe he could turn cat and hide on the streets for a few days to avoid the meeting... but no. **She** could find him anywhere, and he couldn't make her meet with his father alone.

Brigitte brushed two fingers over his hand, snapping him back into the moment in the kitchen. "Kitty?" she said, her voice gentle and worried.

He glanced up, and her face reflected the concern he felt from her.

"Your father isn't going to take you away," she said, soothing him with her calm tones. "He legally can't separate me from my familiar." She scootched her chair closer, wincing when she moved wrong, something he'd seen frequently in the last few days. After a pause and a shuddering breath, she slipped her free hand into his shaggy hair. "Maman, Papa and I will all be prepared to protect you with our magic if we need to. Your father won't be able to overpower us."

"Pretty sure you outclass most of Paris on your own," he said, covering his mouth so the completely inappropriate but borderline hysterical giggles couldn't follow.

"You're not wrong, son," Papa agreed with a smile. "Ling and I aren't exactly light-weights, but..." He shook his head. "Paired with you, our Cupcake is probably one of the most powerful witches in the country." He leaned over and kissed his daughter's cheek. Then he sat and rested a hand on Hēi Māo's neck. "We've got this covered. And while meeting with him tomorrow might be unpleasant, he won't be able to touch you. Not physically, or with his magic."

"I'm going to remove the vestigial magic on your wrists," Brigitte said, patting one gently. "Just in case he can link to it with a compulsion or something."

"Are you sure you're ready for that?" he asked, peering into her face. She wasn't as pale today, but her drowning was all too near and fresh. "Mama can do it, if you're not up for it."

"It shouldn't cause any undue stress," her mama assured him. "She'll be taking a new healing elixir starting this morning to speed things up." She looked him in the eye. "And I'll have a potion for you tonight if you're willing. It'll provide an additional magical barrier should your father try anything tomorrow."

* * *

Hēi Māo carried the small rug from its place in the corner to the sunny center of the room. He could feel the weight of years of spell-work woven into the fabric. It still surprised him that her magic didn't burn the way his father's had; he couldn't even get near his father's casting space without discomfort. He carefully unrolled the round rug before going back for her altar. Normally he'd wait for her cue to set up but she was in no condition to move either of these pieces herself. As her familiar, it was his duty to help, and he was one of few who could touch her magical implements without interfering with her spells. Callie had been tutoring him on his role during Brigitte's naps.

"Thank you, Kitty." She glanced up at him and smiled, before turning back to the wooden chest that occupied the same sacred corner as the rug. She carefully rummaged through the boxes and jars. A gentle clinking accompanied her hand movements as she pulled out what she needed.

"What direction do you want the altar facing?" He hesitated, holding it a few inches off the floor.

Brigitte looked up from her box. Her eyes narrowed slightly before she nodded. "West. It's going to figure more strongly in this spell."

He gently settled it in place. *Let me know if I can do anything else for you.*

"Can you put the candles at the quarters?" she asked holding out four simple white candles and their glass plates.

He eagerly returned to her side and took the supplies. Each candle dish was a different color of clear glass. He stared at them a moment. "The colors matter, don't they?"

Brigitte nodded, giving him a gentle smile. "See if you can figure out where they go. It won't hurt anything if you're wrong and we have to move them."

Was this a test? He wasn't sure he was ready for it. Her hand settled over one of his.

"I'm just curious how sensitive you are to magic," she explained. "I promise, it's okay if you guess wrong."

"Do you have any suggestions to help me?" It probably was a good idea to figure out how clearly he could feel her magic.

"Close your eyes, breathe, and relax," she said.

Crouching over the western point, he closed his eyes and tried to focus on the feeling of the magic emanating from the rug and the candle plates. The blue one seemed the best fit, so he set it down, placing a fat white candle on it. As he worked, Brigitte walked over, moving slower than usual to drape a red cloth over her altar. She dropped a puddle of sheer blue fabric on the altar next to a slim bamboo wand. He had taken his best guess with all the candles by the time she carried over the rest of her supplies. She set down a cauldron, much smaller and less ornate than the one his father used, and slowly knelt at her altar. She closed her eyes and breathed slowly for a moment, and he was certain she was managing her pain, not gathering her magic.

Do you want your medicine? She'd skipped it at breakfast to ensure she was clear-headed for her magic, and he'd worried it was a bad idea.

I'll have it after.

"I can wait, you know," he said, crouching on the opposite side of the altar.

She shook her head, and he could feel her vehement rejection of the idea. "When you see Pierre, you will be free of all his cursed spells." If she'd had more energy, he suspected she would have snarled the words.

"Mama said she could do it," he suggested. He didn't really want to be touched by anyone else's magic, but he'd make an exception for her parents if needed.

141

Her eyes snapped open. "You are **my** familiar, it is my duty and **honor** to do this."

He nodded. "I know. And I appreciate it."

"You've been the victim of magic not of your choosing. Harmful, abusive magic." She scowled.

He smiled, hoping to reassure her. "Your magic is soft and warm."

For a moment, she looked like she might cry. "I'm not going to let anyone else ever touch you with magic without your consent... no, not just consent. It needs to be more enthusiastic than that. Your wholehearted participation." She nodded, apparently satisfied. "I can tell you don't really want Maman to do this. You'd be willing, but that's not enough."

He bowed his head, accepting her decision. "How can I help you?"

She pulled small glass jars and vials out of the cauldron, placing them in the middle of her altar. "We're going to cast the circle together."

He stared at her, shocked. He still knew so little about magic, surely he couldn't, shouldn't do this.

Her hand reached out and brushed his cheek, much as she did when he was in cat form. "Familiars are allowed to help their witches, whether they have any magic of their own or not." She stiffly stood up and glanced at the candles marking the perimeter before turning back to him with a smile. "And you have both your own magic and a pretty good sense for magic, though you haven't been trained."

"I got them right?" That was a pleasant surprise. He'd been in his father's circles of course, but **he** never explained anything, and as he got older Jacque was often blind-folded before his father cast magic on him.

"Good job, Kitty." She held out a white miniature taper,

keeping the matches to herself. "I'll do the casting, but you'll light the candles, okay? I can't bend down well enough."

That made perfect sense. She led him over to the east before lighting her match and touching it to the wick of his candle. As he bent to light the candle placed atop the golden yellow plate, she began.

"I call the guardians of the east, masters of air and new beginnings, to bless this unbinding and fresh start." She wasn't loud, but her voice was clear and confident.

Careful of his lit taper, he knee-walked beside her as she moved widdershins to the northern point. As he ignited the candle on the green plate, she spoke again.

"I call the guardians of the north, masters of earth and prosperity, to bless this unbinding and restoration of free will."

Her hand settled lightly on his head, her fingers in his hair, and he felt calm as the electric build up of her power surrounded them.

"I call the guardians of the west, masters of water and purification, to bless this unbinding and bring forth healing."

Listening carefully to her words as he lit the candle on the blue plate, he understood now why she had chosen to face her altar west. These were the forces she was going to be relying on most heavily in stripping away the remnants of old magic and healing the damage that had been done.

She reached the southern point. "I call the guardians of the south, masters of fire and freedom, to bless the unbinding of this free spirit." She walked him the rest of the way to the east. "The circle is closed, let our workings be blessed."

He felt the completion of the warding, like a pressure in the middle of his forehead. Then she directed him to sit across from her, pointing to the candle-holder mounted to the side of the cluttered altar. He pushed the candle into place and settled on his knees as she waited. The whole space felt warm and soft, like the most comfortable sunbeam in the history of sunbeams.

"We stand outside of time and place, on the threshold of never and always to strip away bonds that were given without consent and with unkind intent." Her voice was low, solemn. It was a stark contrast to the joyful way she completed the familiar ceremony and the urgent supplication when she banished the demon.

He watched as she picked up a very sharp ceremonial knife, a red Chinese knot dangling from the handle. She held up a fragment of tree bark before shaving it into slivers, dropping them into the tiny cauldron. Next, she opened a jar and plucked out the round disk of a dried fiddle-head fern. After holding it out for him to see, she crushed it between her palms so the fragments joined the bark. She picked up a brown vial with a neat label declaring it betony. The moment the top was off, its scent hit the air, reminding him vaguely of mint. She tilted it to let two drops fall into the cauldron.

Drawing a slow breath, Brigitte picked up the bamboo wand and the little white taper. She used the wand to stir the contents of the cauldron before tipping the candle in to ignite the mixture. Blue and red sparkles floated up instead of smoke. She set aside the candle again. When she waved her hand over the mixture, he felt her power, pouring out of her fingertips. She stirred again, then tapped the bamboo three times against the little round belly of the cauldron. She picked up the blue fabric he'd noticed earlier. It was long and narrow, like a scarf, and she slowly fed it into the cauldron like some strange inverted sleight of hand trick. She gathered the knife and bottles off the altar and patted the surface.

Hands here, please.

He lightly placed his hands on the altar without even thinking. Building up to this point had been easy, but he suddenly realized she was about to work magic **on** him, and he gasped, nervous. He could feel his pulse throbbing in his neck.

I won't hurt you, Kitty, she whispered into his mind. *I won't ever hurt you with my magic.*

He met her eyes. There was still so much he didn't know about magic, so much he needed to learn to be a good familiar.

She rested her hands on his for a moment, her fingertips brushing at his wrists. *Let's remove that for good.*

He nodded.

Three more taps to the little cauldron and a puff of pink smoke burst out. She reached in and pulled out the scarf with her fingertips. He gawked at the faint glow of magic on the fabric.

Is something wrong? she asked, hesitating with the length of voile held aloft but not touching him.

I can see your magic. I've never seen magic before. Felt it, smelled it, even tasted it, but never seen it. Had her power continued to grow as they got to know each other? He remembered Papa mentioning something about familiars and witches getting used to each other and gaining new skills, but he hadn't expected anything like this.

Does it hurt your eyes?

He shook his head. *It's beautiful.*

With a single nod, she continued with her spell, wrapping one end around each of his wrists. While it gave a faint sensation of being bound, he knew he could pull away if he wanted to. Holding her hands over his wrists, she closed her eyes. "I strip away the magics placed against your will." She wiggled her fingers a little. "I expunge even the barest trace of the efforts to bend you against your nature. I return your full freedom as an independent entity of this plane."

She reached into the cauldron and pulled out a pinch of what would have been ash if her magic hadn't transformed it to a sparkly fine powder. She sprinkled it over his fabric-wrapped wrists. Dipping three fingers from each hand into the little pot, she reached out and drew them over his cheeks in three lines out from his nose toward his ears. She grinned at him, and he realized she'd anointed him with sparkly magical whiskers. Was magic supposed to be fun? His father was always so stern and serious about it.

"So purified, I request a boon of healing and happiness upon this shape-shifter, that the remainder of his life balances the hardships he's borne."

He closed his eyes, feeling the soothing warmth of her magic washing over him.

Brigitte deftly slipped the fabric off his wrists, tossing it into the air. She snapped her fingers and it vanished in a puff of flame. "So it has been commanded, so it is done."

He felt lighter now somehow. Though he'd done much to destroy the remainders of his father's spells, the remnants had worn on him more than he realized. It was a relief to be truly free, and he smiled when he realized that by binding himself as a familiar, he'd managed to gain true freedom.

"Depart in peace, benevolent guardians. We humbly thank you for your aid and protection," Brigitte murmured, banishing the circle and dousing the candles in an arcane breeze.

He felt the magic drop, but the lightness inside him remained.

"How do you feel, Kitty?" she asked, peering into his face. "I thought you were doing okay, but..."

He nodded. "That was nice... actually." He looked down at his hands on the altar. "Really nice." He smiled shyly at her. "Your magic is soft and safe. I really like it."

"I'm glad." She sighed, looking a little tired. "You generally won't have to help me with magic like this, not if you don't want to."

"But I'll be allowed to help if I want to?" he asked eagerly. With the little tastes he'd gotten of **her** formal magic, he wanted to participate.

"Of course," she agreed. "Whenever you'd like to."

"Can I get your medicine so you can nap?" he asked. "I can clean up for you." He saw the glint of hope, before she tried to squash it with her sense of duty. "Really. I want to. And it's my job to help you. Let me do my job."

She let out a little laugh. "Okay, Kitty. You win."

Chapter Twenty-Seven

Their lawyer, Madame Chien was able to put off Pierre Parenteau another four days. Which meant Brigitte was still quite sore, but not so exhausted, and Hēi Māo had shoes that fit by that time. They met at the law office, because Hēi Māo had advised against letting his father pick the location. The man apparently had a knack for using anything he could find against those who opposed him. The conference room held an air of importance, reinforced by high-backed leather chairs, a shiny oval table, and dark woodwork.

Monsieur Parenteau breezed into the room at exactly three. He stood near the doorway, surveying the room and its occupants as though assessing their worth. "Come Jacque," he called. "It's time to go home." There was no warmth in his voice, no relief at the sight of his son healthy and well.

"No," Hēi Māo said calmly. "I'm not going with you."

Monsieur Parenteau looked surprised. "Come, Jacque," he repeated, and this time Brigitte felt his magic looking for something.

"I'm sorry, sir. Your bindings aren't on him anymore," Brigitte said. "Your magic won't stick."

Monsieur Parenteau looked at her in surprise, and she felt

148

him drop his seeking.

"I'm sure you're aware that it's unethical to tamper with another witch's spells," he said tightly, his expression going to her parents as if expecting them to chastise her.

Brigitte nodded. "As I'm sure you're aware of the **modern** ethical concerns with binding sentient beings contrary to their nature." She wasn't even supposed to be talking. Her parents and the lawyer could take hold of the conversation any time now. His eyes narrowed, but she spoke again before he could. "Either way, I didn't touch your spells. None of us did. They were in tatters when I found Hēi Māo."

"Hēi Māo?" He gave his son a more intensive look this time. "You let her find you in **cat** form? Are you a **complete** idiot? What did you think I was trying to protect you from?"

She felt Hēi Māo's hand wrap around hers under the table as she started to bristle at the implied accusation that she'd forced his son into his role as familiar.

"I picked her," Hēi Māo said. "Not the other way around."

"And you've let her make a **pet** of you, by the look of it," he snapped gesturing toward Hēi Māo's neck.

"Have you got a familiar, Monsieur Parenteau?" Already knowing the answer, Brigitte didn't give him time to reply before moving on. "Hēi Māo is no mere pet, and he's not a passing fancy. He chose to become my familiar, free of bindings or drugs or lies." Hēi Māo still didn't truly understand that she bent to his needs as much as he bent to hers, but in time he would. It hurt her that being treated with kindness and respect still surprised him, but she could see why now.

"As you know, Monsieur Parenteau," Madame Chien finally broke in. "A familiar contract is by its very nature legally binding and unbreakable. By arcane canon law, which has been consistently upheld by civil law, Jacque Parenteau now belongs to Brigitte

Defresne-Li."

"In that case, I insist both children be relocated to my family home, so Jacque can continue being raised according to his social class," Pierre said firmly. "This does not interfere with their... contract." He made the word sound like something disgusting. "And it takes into consideration that he has not been reared to the simple lifestyle of a baker's family." While his eyes darted, he didn't quite look at Brigitte's parents.

She felt Hēi Māo's indignation a moment before he spoke. "I was a stray cat for five months. I assure you, the simple life of fresh bread and a warm bed is superior to hunting vermin and sleeping in cramped spaces behind heating ducts." He shrugged. "Though to be fair, rat isn't half bad." This statement silenced the room. Brigitte saw her papa desperately trying to hold in a laugh while Monsieur Parenteau put a hand to his mouth to stifle a gag. He'd been her idol once, the designer she wanted to be like. Now she wanted to be nothing like him.

"We will continue to live with my parents," Brigitte stated firmly. "I appreciate your concern for my familiar's comfort, and while it's true he will not have some of the material benefits he had under your roof, he has been thriving without them. He will enroll in school when I return to classes, so we are seeing to his education as well."

"He is a internationally famous model and the heir of a wealthy family," Monsieur Parenteau snapped. "Has it ever occurred to you that he has been the target of abductions for ransom in the past?"

Brigitte smiled. "I'm capable of containing and banishing seventh circle demons with about thirty seconds warning and no backup. Hēi Māo and I have acquired full telepathic abilities with each other. A witch can always find her familiar; the same can not be said for a parent and their child."

* * *

Hēi Māo was suddenly assaulted by the terrible thought of Brigitte bound and gagged in his father's wine cellar. "The reverse is also true," Hēi Māo added quietly. He wasn't sure if his father would try to do something to her, but it wouldn't surprise him, and he wanted it clear from the start that he would always find her.

"He is safer now than he has ever been," Brigitte said. Her hand moved to lightly brush Hēi Māo's wrist, where she'd removed the last hints of the manacles.

"Have we heard all of your concerns regarding this issue, Monsieur?" Madame Chien asked.

His father collected himself and addressed her parents. "Are you prepared to care for my son, should your little business fail?" Everything in his posture and tone set off Hēi Māo's warning bells.

"Is that a threat?" Mama asked, her quiet voice somehow far deadlier and more intimidating than his father's boldest blustering. It was impressive, and he was delighted to see it directed at his father.

"Of course not," his father said, not even trying to sound sincere. "I just want to be sure you are prepared for all contingencies."

Hēi Māo would have liked to roll his eyes at the lies and the dramatics, but thought it best to maintain some semblance of propriety.

"Our profits may not compare to yours, but our **little** business is very successful," Papa said.

As the meeting dragged on, Hēi Māo worried that the issue was less cut-and-dried than he'd been told. He fought against the desire to turn cat and climb into the ductwork.

"If I may?" Brigitte interjected.

"The adults are talking now, child," his father snapped. "Kindly hold your tongue."

Before Hēi Māo could let out the entirely feline hiss blocking his throat, Madame Chien held up a hand. "Monsieur Parenteau, I will remind you that by arcane canon law, Brigitte has reached the age of majority. And as all of this discussion concerns her familiar, her voice is relevant." She sighed, setting her hand down. "If we can't come to an agreement here, we will have to involve a judge and mediation. France has never had a legal case of this nature; in fact it may be entirely unique internationally. I expect it would be extremely newsworthy." She gave his father a long stare. "Are you willing to endure the media circus?"

"Hēi Māo wants to keep this civil, and I'm happy to go along with that," Brigitte said, and he could tell she was trying to defuse the situation with her words. "If we work together, and do it now, we can develop a cover story that satisfies all our needs."

His father continued to scowl at Brigitte, but it seemed less hostile somehow.

"You haven't enjoyed having him at home with you," she said gently. "This fixes that situation."

"His condition will get out," his father said flatly.

Hēi Māo glared at him. It wasn't a condition. It was his nature. It couldn't be treated or changed, and he wouldn't have wanted a cure even if it were possible.

Brigitte nodded. "At this point, it's going to get out anyway. Why not do it on your terms instead of as some reporter's scoop?"

"And I suppose **you** have a suggestion, Mademoiselle Defresne-Li," his father said snidely.

"I know something of the fashion industry, and a little about the news," she said.

Hēi Māo would have liked to point out that she was also brilliant, but held his tongue.

"I think it would be in your best interest to appear supportive of shape-shifters. You married one, and your son is another, after all," Brigitte explained. "No one will believe you didn't know about either of them at this point. But it would be reasonable and compassionate if you kept quiet to protect them. If you were concerned about the bias against their people."

"You want me to use my business as a platform for shape-shifter support?" his father demanded, sounding more irritated than disgusted.

"It would be more bold than Vianne's floral and striped collection from this past spring," she assured him.

"**That** was a travesty," his father muttered.

"It was quite hideous," Brigitte agreed. "But it was bold. And it launched her small label into the ring with the big houses."

It had taken some work to get her to agree to his suggestions on their cover story. It had to fit their needs while appealing to his father and his urge to appear superior to his son.

"Hēi Māo is okay with claiming to have had some sort of cultural identity crisis, to explain why he vanished and how he ended up with me. With no shifters to get guidance from, he went to explore is cat side and… things happened." She looked calm, but he could still tell she hated the idea.

His father sighed, looking sullen. "You've stolen my best model," he said, most of the fight gone from his voice. "Do you have a solution for that?"

Hēi Māo suddenly realized how he could give back to her for all she'd done, and would continue to do, for him. He wasn't trying to level the playing field, really. It just seemed fair for him to do something that would benefit her, especially when it was so easy for him to do. "I'd be willing to continue modeling for you," he said quietly.

"You would?" his father asked, suspicious.

"But no more than one shoot per week," he added. He wanted it to be a very part time thing. "I'm going to be going to school, so I'll need to be able to study."

"What about runway?" his father asked, in full negotiation mode. "Fashion week is critical to the business, and it's not a one-day affair."

Hēi Māo nodded. "I'll walk runway for you under one condition."

"If it's about your salary, I'd expect to keep it the same for another year, then it should take a steep jump up, if you keep in shape of course."

Hēi Māo shook his head. "For every two designs of yours I show, I get to wear one of my Brigitte's." He'd seen her work, and while he was no designer, he'd spent his entire life around fashion. She was already as good as, if not better than his father. She just lacked experience, exposure, and access to the business side.

"What?" Brigitte demanded looking at him. "What are you doing?"

"Do you have design samples available?" his father asked, glancing over Brigitte. "I assume you made that dress and jacket, did you not?"

"Well..." She glanced at her clothes. "Yes, but..."

He arched one eyebrow. "You're a designer. Surely you have your book, or some examples on your phone."

Show him your book. Hēi Māo looked at her, throwing her the most intense kitten eyes he could manage in his human form. *Please. Trust me. This will help both of us in the end.*

With a resigned sigh, Brigitte lifted her small messenger bag from the floor and pulled out her current design book. She flipped past a few pages before sliding it across the table.

"Hmmm," his father muttered, peering over the sketches on several pages before straightening and closing the cover. He couldn't help but notice that his father handed it back with a level of respect he'd never seen before. Turning back to Hēi Māo, he

154

resumed their negotiation. "I must have final choice in the designs."

Hēi Māo nodded. "She'll show you what she's working on, and you'll pick from those."

"Done." His father got to his feet. "Please send me the final draft of our agreement by tomorrow afternoon, Madame Chien. I would like to make a statement to the public in the next few days, and that should be signed first." He nodded to Mama and Papa. "Monsieur and Madame Defresne-Li, my assistant will contact you with Jacque's medical records and my contact information should you need to reach me." With that, he left, and Hēi Māo relaxed in his chair.

Brigitte turned to him, her face worried. "Why would you do that?"

He shifted back to cat and hopped into her lap. *You help me. This way I could help you too.*

Chapter Twenty-Eight

The day after meeting with Pierre, Brigitte texted Ruhul and Aalia asking them to bring her homework, and plan to stay for dinner. She mentioned that there was something important they needed to know, and she wanted them to hear it from her.

"Gitte!" Ruhul called as he came up the stairs. "We're coming up. You'd better be decent."

"Don't yell," Aalia admonished. "She's been sick. She could be sleeping."

Brigitte was stretched out on her chaise with Hēi Māo in cat form on her lap when they came in. She'd talked to him about how he wanted to handle this. She knew her friends would like him, and he needed friends. But he was nervous and wanted to work up to it.

"I'd give you the biggest hug, but your mama said you're really sore," Aalia said. "What happened?"

"Oh, it's so good to see you two," Brigitte said, keeping one hand running over Hēi Māo's back. "Have a seat."

"You okay?" Ruhul asked, dragging over one of the desk chairs.

Brigitte nodded. "Did you guys hear about that seventh circle demon that went on a rampage last week?"

"You were one of the victims?" Aalia looked horrified, her face paler than her friends had ever seen. "Oh, Gitte..."

"I'm okay. Honest." She reached under the blanket and pulled out some folded black fabric. She was moving better now, but she wasn't up for anything strenuous. "But, um... you've seen the video, right?"

When they both nodded, she flicked out the fabric, unfolding and twisting it so they could see the black and yellow pattern. Her mother had washed the capelet, returning it a few days after the attack.

"Holy shit," Ruhul whispered. "You... you're..."

"You're Mademoiselle Butterfly!" Aalia squealed. "Gitte, you're freaking amazing."

"You almost died." Ruhul sounded like he felt queasy.

"I promise, I'm fine." Brigitte reached out to pat his knee. "But... um. Yeah. I guess my magic is pretty strong now."

"Gitte, most witches **never** get strong enough to take on seventh circle demons without help," Ruhul pointed out, his eyes bulging. "You're like, the biggest gun."

She gestured to Hēi Māo. "I had help. I mean... that's what having a familiar can do. I'm still me." She briefly worried her magic ability had crossed over from cool to creepy.

"You're still our girl," Aalia reassured her.

"Our freakishly strong girl," Ruhul added.

"But I did drown, and CPR is... it's hard on the ribs."

"So that's why we can't squeeze you," Aalia said in realization. "Your mama warned us, but she was pretty vague."

Brigitte nodded.

"Did you hear about who they think rescued you?" Aalia asked. "It's all speculation right now, but there's some pretty good photo evidence that you were rescued by **Jacque Parenteau**."

"Yeah," Brigitte bit her lip and looked at Hēi Māo. *Ready?*

Ready, he confirmed, moving to a clear spot on the chaise.

"I was, only he doesn't like being called that anymore." She moved to sit up a bit more, wincing a little. "We're going to show you something, and tell you something that you can't tell anyone yet. It'll be public knowledge before I come back to school, but we want you two to know now."

Her friends nodded, quietly promising the safety of her secret.

"Hēi Māo's not an ordinary cat," Brigitte said.

"That's not a surprise," Ruhul said. "Even for a familiar he's..." He faltered, realization dawning on his face. "Is **he**...?"

"Okay, Kitty," Brigitte encouraged.

The green light of his change flashed, and suddenly a green-eyed blond boy sat next to her, his hand creeping nervously closer to hers.

"Hēi Māo is a shape-shifter," Brigitte said. "He ran away from home because his father is... neither a shape-shifter nor at all understanding of shape-shifters." She took a slow, careful breath. "I'd kind of like to send him where I sent that demon, actually," she mumbled.

Hēi Māo laughed.

"He planned to stay a cat for the rest of his life, and after seeing me looking for a familiar, he decided he should try that instead of being a stray."

"I'm the best familiar ever," he said quietly.

"**Obviously**." Brigitte rolled her eyes. Getting to know him outside his cat form made her fully realize how much he craved affection.

Aalia was staring at Hēi Māo, her mouth slightly open. "Gitte, your familiar is a supermodel."

"I'd like it if you two could be friends with him, too," Brigitte said. "I don't know how either of you feel about a boy who is also a literal cat, but... he could use some good friends, and you two **are** the best there are."

Ruhul gave her a sweet smile. "Like you had to ask, Gitte." He held out a fist to Hēi Māo. "Pleased to properly make your acquaintance, cat-dude."

Hēi Māo stared at the fist uncertainly for a moment, until Brigitte prompted him. *It's allowed, if you want to do it.*

Hēi Māo beamed at Ruhul and bumped his fist.

"What do you want to be called?" Aalia asked.

"You two can still call me Hēi Māo if you want, since that's the name we met by." He beamed at Ruhul. "Cat-dude is good, too. I've never had nicknames before."

"We're going with Tom Hēi as his new official name, it's what he'll use at school, and he's going to continue to model under the new name, though we aren't legally changing it right now. His... father will be releasing a statement about that soon."

* * *

Once he'd been reintroduced to her friends, and their questions had been answered, he watched her expertly steer them back to more routine topics. They'd probably all had enough drama for the day... or month, really. He'd be content living the rest of his life without another magical fight of some sort.

"Did you guys bring our homework?" Hēi Māo asked.

"Really?" Aalia demanded, holding her hands up in the air in disbelief. "You want to do homework, **now**?"

"Brigitte's very diligent," Hēi Māo pointed out. He knew she was worried about getting so far behind she'd have trouble catching up.

"Really?" Aalia raised an eyebrow in disbelief, though he thought she was teasing.

"Hey, way to kick me while I'm down," Brigitte said, pouting. "I'll have you know that my grades have been up since I got my familiar. Despite the drop that most witch-born experience during their adjustment."

"You have a built-in tutor." Ruhul smiled at Hēi Māo. "Are you going to start school with us, too?"

Hēi Māo nodded eagerly, his hands gripping his knees. "I've never been to school before. Well, other than as Brigitte's familiar, so that'll be different."

Aalia gawked at him in surprise. "Never? Isn't that illegal? Education is compulsory in France."

"I was homeschooled," he explained. "Teachers came to me." It was true, but it was really only half the story.

You don't have to share anything you aren't ready for, Brigitte whispered into his mind.

"Plenty of wealthy families do that," Ruhul said. "Hell, I've often wondered why the mayor didn't just hire tutors for Celeste. Would've been nicer for all of us."

"She's changed a lot," Hēi Māo said, looking down at the floor when he felt all their eyes turn to him. He wouldn't have recognized her if not for hearing her name from the detective and on the news.

"Do you **know** Celeste?" Brigitte asked.

He worried that he should have mentioned it earlier, and it made him wonder what else he'd failed to tell her. "I did, but not anymore." He shook his head. "When both our moms were still around, we played together often." He shrugged. "She attacked you, unprovoked, and that's... it's not something she would've done when we were kids."

"She nearly killed you," Brigitte said, suddenly a whole lot more subdued.

"And you saved me," he insisted. He flashed her a happy

smile. "You're saving me a lot these days. It's becoming a habit."

She snorted. "Yeah, well you've saved me, too. So we're even."

"To answer your question," Ruhul said, "I brought your homework, and Aalia and I would be happy to help you out. We've already shared our class notes with you."

"I'll help with Mandarin and physics," Hēi Māo offered. He liked those classes.

"Thank god," Aalia said. "Neither of us took Mandarin, and I consider just passing physics enough."

"He could help you too," Brigitte suggested. "He's really good at it."

"I'm so glad you're not just a cat," Ruhul said with a swift shake of his head. "I was starting to feel incredibly stupid next to you."

It was such an unexpected and normal sentiment that Hēi Māo let out a laugh. He'd overheard enough when modeling and seen plenty on TV to know that both non-magic people and witch-born generally distrusted shape-shifters. Film, TV and book villains were disproportionally shape-shifters, and they were all too frequently the punchline of jokes and comedic routines. He worried about going public with his nature; Brigitte was powerful enough to keep him safe, but could he do the same for her?

"You... you don't mind that I'm a shape-shifter?" he asked.

Ruhul shook his head. "I've never understood why other people are so nasty about shifters. You're magic, so are witch-born. And no magic is inherently bad, it's all how we use it." He reached out, hesitating over Hēi Māo's shoulder.

"It's okay, Ruhul," Brigitte said.

"So weird," Ruhul whispered, then he patted Hēi Māo's shoulder twice. "I've got your back, dude. You're my friend, and I liked you even when you were just a cat. Gitte's been happier and more confident since she found you, and that says a lot about you."

Warmth suffused Hēi Māo, washing away the last traces of anxiety that had built up while he waited to reveal himself to them.

"I'd love to learn more about you and shape-shifters in general, so I understand you better," Ruhul added.

"That brings up a really good point," Aalia said quickly. "Hēi Māo, if we do or say something that's offensive, even a little bit, you tell us, okay? Because we won't learn and fix it if we don't know."

"That goes for me, too," Brigitte said, gently rubbing his back. *Our relationship is too important to risk on you being polite if I hurt you.*

"Thanks," Hēi Māo said, his vision getting a little blurry. "You're amazing, and I'm honored you want to be friends with me. I'm going to like getting to know you better, too."

At dinner, Hēi Māo got to see more directly how Brigitte's friends were treated as family.

"How's school going?" Papa asked, as he handed Ruhul the bread basket.

"It's been a pretty good year for me so far," Ruhul replied. He held the basket out toward Hēi Māo. "I'm getting to do some really neat stuff in my music theory class, and that's where I'm focusing my energy."

"That's fantastic," Papa said, nodding. "You've always had a particularly strong connection between your magic and your music."

While Hēi Māo had been part of game night a couple of times, this sort of dinner was new to him. He liked seeing how Nik and Ling made an effort to truly know Brigitte's friends. Their approach to him had seemed unrealistic, but now he understood that it was just how they were.

"How about you, Aalia," Nik asked. "Still doing the school paper?"

"She's editor, now," Brigitte said, beaming at her friend.

Aalia laughed. "Yeah. And it's going really well. Madame Bouvier thinks we may get nominated for some awards for excellence in *lycée* journalism if we keep up the quality we've got going this year."

"It's so nice to see you kids finding your niches, and really showing off what you're capable of," Mama said, sounding as proud of them as she was of her daughter.

"Any idea what activities you'll want to try out, cat-dude?" Ruhul asked, looking at Hēi Māo.

Hēi Māo shook his head, feeling a bit panicked. Should he know? Should he be researching?

"No worries," Ruhul said, his attitude of relaxed calm somehow spread to Hēi Māo. "We'll help you find your interests."

Chapter Twenty-Nine

Hēi Māo peeked out of his sling as Brigitte walked toward the alley where he'd most often visited with Miss Gigi. He reached out of his safe haven to point at a blue door. *That one. The one with the diviner sign over the post box.*

Brigitte pressed the bell. He could hear the gentle chime from within. After several moments there were rushing footsteps and the door opened.

"Good afternoon!" A tall thin woman stood on the other side of the threshold, dressed in bright colors and wearing crystal jewelry. She had pale skin and light brown hair. "How may I help you?"

"We're here to see Miss Gigi," Brigitte said, patting the sling lightly.

The woman seemed a bit startled. "Miss Gigi?" She looked down and noticed Hēi Māo's face peering up at her. "Oh, hello. Are you friends with my Miss Gigi?"

"She helped me when I was looking for a familiar of my own," Brigitte explained. "She brought me all the local strays she could round up."

164

"Oh!" The woman clasped her hands together. "Yes. She told me that she was helping someone." She stepped back and gestured for them to enter. "Please come in. My name is Ines."

"I'm Brigitte, and this is Tom." She patted the sling again.

"That's a fabulous carrier," Ines said. "Wherever did you find it?"

Hēi Māo chose that moment to climb out, demonstrating the padded shoulder, where he perched.

"Oooh," Ines gushed. "Such a clever design."

"I made it, actually," Brigitte said, and he could hear the pride in her voice. "And I'd be happy to make one for you and Miss Gigi. I feel I owe you both a great debt."

Ines waved the words away as she led them into the living room. "We both enjoy helping others, I assure you, it's not that great a thing."

Brigitte shook her head. "It really was." She sat on the couch, and Hēi Māo hopped down beside her. "She convinced Tom to consider the life of a familiar. He'd seen me several times, but avoided meeting me on principle."

Hēi Māo stretched up and bumped his forehead under her chin. *I didn't know what I was passing up.*

Brigitte's hand ran over his back. *You'd been intentionally mislead.* She looked up at their hostess. "She didn't coerce him or anything," she insisted. "She just helped him understand what this life could be like."

She could see we were a good match, Hēi Māo said.

Brigitte smiled and nodded. "I guess she told him that she could see what kind of witch I was, and how we would complement each other."

"Oh." Ines beamed at them. "She's very good at that."

Miss Gigi pranced in then, her well-groomed coat bouncing and swaying with her movement. She paused when she saw Hēi

Māo sitting on the couch beside the witch she'd encouraged him to meet.

"So you did go home with her," Miss Gigi said, her words for Hēi Māo alone. "It looks to have done you well."

"It has," he agreed, speaking in cat. "And I am grateful for your guidance."

"Does she fully know what you are yet?" Miss Gigi asked.

Hēi Māo nodded. "And it has changed nothing though I probably should have revealed it to her before we bonded." He understood now that he'd made a mistake with that, but trading service for safety had seemed such a good idea at the time.

"Hello again, Miss Gigi," Brigitte said aloud for all to hear. "Tom and I wanted to thank you for your help earlier this fall." She held out a gift bag. "You were so kind to help me find the available cats and kittens. And I know he wouldn't have chosen to even consider me if you hadn't spoken with him."

Miss Gigi took obvious delight in tugging out the tissue paper.

"Why was he so averse to becoming a familiar?" Ines asked, watching Miss Gigi dismantle the packaging with enthusiasm.

Brigitte sighed. For now they weren't sharing his full nature with everyone, but she'd know it eventually. "He'd been purposefully misinformed and mistreated. His experiences with magic were extremely unpleasant."

Ines' face drooped as she looked at Hēi Māo now. "I'm so sorry for your past experiences, Tom."

Tell her I'm the happiest I've ever been, he said.

Brigitte repeated his words, adding, "I make a point to do right by him. And he's such a wonderful familiar."

Done with the wrappings for now, Miss Gigi pulled out each bag of treats, baked by Brigitte last night, and placed them on the coffee table.

"This is a small token of our appreciation," Brigitte said,

gesturing to the treats. "And I'd really love to make you a sling like mine, if it's something you'd enjoy."

Ines nodded. "Miss Gigi and I would like that." She reached over and patted Brigitte's hand. "And my dear, I think it would be wonderful to get to know you and Tom more."

Chapter Thirty

"It's just down the street here," Brigitte said, catching Hēi Māo's hand and tugging him down the sidewalk. Even with the thin gloves they wore, he felt a hint of warmth from his witch's touch.

"It looks smaller," he pointed out, grinning at her. "But that happens." He found it natural and easy to extrapolate from one perspective to the other, and he wondered if that was a shape-shifter ability, or if it was a particular talent of his.

He'd been surprised with how much more relaxed and happy he was, now that he didn't have to hide in cat form. It wasn't about being a person or a cat; it was about having the choice. He especially liked being in cat shape at night and on the subway.

"So this is it?" she asked, pointing to Master Fu's sign, written in both French and Chinese.

He nodded and held a little tighter to her as they walked up the few steps. He hesitated at the door, oddly nervous. Brigitte reached out to pull it open.

"Master Fu?" she called. "Are you in?"

"Ah ha," the older man's voice carried from a side room. "Good morning, Brigitte." The tiny Chinese man came out of the

168

room and bowed, greeting them. He had straight silvery hair and wore a red and white Hawaiian shirt. "Or should I say Mademoiselle Butterfly and Tom?" He chuckled, patting his hands together. "I've never been visited by superheroes before."

Hēi Māo had always felt Master Fu knew more than he let on. He wondered how the man knew she was Mademoiselle Butterfly and he was the stray cat who'd visited. Because his father had used very cautious wording in his press release about Jacque's disposition, their full story wouldn't be public for a few more days. Mama had a well-known reporter friend who was scheduled to interview them for that part.

"So you recognize Tom, then?" Brigitte asked, and he was grateful she was comfortable handling such things.

Master Fu nodded, smiling broadly at Hēi Māo. "When you stopped coming by, I'd hoped you'd found yourself a nice home."

"I did," Hēi Māo agreed.

"The home of Ling Li and Tom Defresne would be a perfect fit for you." Master Fu nodded. "I admit I tried to direct Brigitte to you when I learned she was looking for a familiar. Your chi patterns are nicely matched; did you know that?"

Hēi Māo shook his head. "I can't see chi."

"It's not one of my gifts either," Brigitte admitted.

Master Fu tilted his head a bit. "Ling can see chi colors, but you have your own special gifts, my dear. And as for you, Tom, I suspect you just need some instruction. Shape-shifters tend to be quite adept, cats especially so."

He had never entertained the idea that he could have some form of magic beyond his ability to inflict misfortune. He glanced at his witch for a moment, temporarily stunned to silence.

"I wanted to thank you for taking care of Tom before I found him," Brigitte said, bowing.

Master Fu waved her off. "Nonsense. It was only once in a

while, and it was nice to have someone to talk to." He leaned toward Hēi Māo. "You were such a good listener. I could tell you were always paying attention, even when I wandered off on a tangent. Or when I switched to Mandarin." He grinned. "You would make a good student."

"How did you know I was a shape-shifter?" Hēi Māo asked. "I mean, you seemed to know, and you're not surprised."

The elderly Chinese man laughed. "You are a **very** convincing cat, young Tom. But I'm extremely well acquainted with shape-shifters, being one myself."

"You can turn into a cat, too?" Hēi Māo blurted, his pulse suddenly racing.

"Tortoise, actually," he said, shrugging. "Not quite as useful in Paris as a cat, but there's a reason I spend the coldest weeks of winter somewhere at the beach." He winked. "I also knew your mother, so that helped. You're obviously her kitten."

"Oh," Brigitte whispered.

"Nik and Ling were among the first Parisians to accept me when I moved here, so I knew they'd keep you safe," Master Fu added. "And I see that they've done that, and some."

Hēi Māo stared at the man, feeling like he'd been put in a dark box and shaken, while in cat form. His senses had all gone numb and disorientation washed over him. Brigitte ushered him into a small room, settling him on a cushion. Her hand moved in his hair the same way it did in his coat when he was a cat, soothing him.

It's okay, she whispered in his mind. *I'm here. You're safe. We'll help you.*

Her voice and touch were the only things anchoring him, and he knew he would have been lost without her. His other senses slowly returned. A soft chime rang out at regular intervals, accompanied by a low humming. They were good to focus on. He could smell tea, not the kind Brigitte drank, but he'd picked up hints of it in the kitchen from time to time.

"Aaah, you're back with us then, young Tom," Master Fu said, his voice warm and reassuring. "I didn't mean to shock you like that."

"It's…" He faltered at the frog in his throat, clearing it gruffly. "It's okay." Brigitte offered him a hand, and he took it, grateful and desperate at the same time. "You really know my mother?"

Master Fu nodded. "I haven't seen her in years, of course. I'm fairly certain she's not even in Paris."

Hēi Māo nodded. Sure he'd be disappointed about that later, but utterly lacked the emotional capacity at the moment.

"But I'd be happy to introduce you to other shape-shifters, including family you've never met," Master Fu offered. "It's possible we can find someone who knows where she ended up. They may have ways to contact her that currently elude me."

"I have family?" Unexpected hope blossomed in his chest. "You really think we could really find her?"

"I do." Master Fu nodded. "For some time after she left the Parenteau household, I saw her regularly, and I have some ideas about who to talk to and where to start." He held up a hand as if in caution. "This will take time. I don't think she **chose** to leave her home and her kitten, so our approach will need to be cautious and our methods less direct to avoid detection by others."

"Okay." He nodded eagerly.

"And perhaps while we work on that, I can help you identify where your magic skills lay," Master Fu added. "I'm certain there's more than your ability to cast misfortune, though that can be a strong power if you train yourself to use it properly."

Chapter Thirty-One

Hēi Māo felt Brigitte's nervousness through their bond. It surprised him that she could face his father without showing a hint of jitters, but this interview, with a family friend, had her all worked up. *You're going to do great*, he told her, wanting to reassure her as she'd done for him at times.

She nodded her acknowledgment, but didn't respond as she hung her coat where the studio coordinator directed them. The woman was gushing about how exciting it was to get the exclusive first interview with Jacque Parenteau.

He felt his witch flinch every time the woman mentioned his name. Her reaction, the fact that she noticed and cared about it so much warmed him. *It's okay. They don't know.*

You don't use that name. It's not who you are anymore, not who you ever wanted to be. Her distress was palpable.

He smiled at her, knowing his happiness was clear on his face. *Soon everyone will know that's not who I am anymore, and that I belong to you.*

Her anxiousness faded and she shot him a look. *We belong to each other.*

It was only in the last few days that he came to truly grasp how much she meant that last bit. He'd known from the start that she respected him and considered him a partner, not property. It was only now, that he understood. *We belong to each other*, he agreed.

"Brigitte!" a woman called. "It's lovely to see you!" He recognized her as the news anchor Nala Freis. She embraced his witch. "Thank you so much for giving me this interview."

Brigitte smiled, clearly feeling more at ease. "I wouldn't have wanted to do this with anyone else. I know you'll handle it with the sensitivity it requires."

The woman's eyes went wide, and he could imagine all the thoughts running through her head. As a journalist, she was sure to find the most sensational angles to every story. She turned to Hēi Māo then. "And Jacque, it's a pleasure to meet you." She nodded to him but didn't reach out to shake his hand, so apparently that request had been passed along and was being taken seriously.

"Thank you, Madame Freis," he said, flashing one of his bright model smiles. "I'm just glad you were able to fit us in so quickly."

Within minutes, he and Brigitte were sitting on a couch across from the journalist. It felt more comfortable than most of the sets he'd been on in the past.

"With brilliant hues, it's Paris news," Nala declared, turned toward stage center as the cameras started rolling. "I'm your host Nala Freis, and I'm joined today by Paris' darling, Jacque Parenteau, who went missing following a photo shoot in June. He's here with Brigitte Defresne-Li to share the story of where he's been and what's changed for him." She turned to them. "Welcome, Jacque and Brigitte."

"Thanks for having us, Nala," Brigitte said.

"We appreciate you taking the time to talk with us," he said.

They'd practiced interviewing each other and rehearsed a bit with Aalia and Ruhul so they were ready with what they wanted to share.

"The pleasure is mine," Nala insisted. "So where does this story start? How did you two meet?"

Brigitte looked at him. *This one's yours.*

He nodded. "We met in September, but that's not really the best starting point. For that, we need to go back to June, when I went missing."

Nala nodded encouragingly.

"I've had a lot of people ask me why I would suddenly abandon my home and a thriving career, and the truth is that I'm not entirely as I seem." He was glad they didn't have a studio audience, because even with just two camera techs and the folks in the sound booth, he could feel the rising tension. "While my father is witch-born, my mother was a shape-shifter." There was a collective gasp, and Brigitte's hand came to rest gently between his shoulder blades. "Given the way my people are viewed, this obviously couldn't be public knowledge, and my father worked to keep my nature under wraps." He felt Brigitte bristling at the half truth. "Without my mother's help, he was really only equipped to raise the human side of Jacque Parenteau."

Nala leaned forward, clearly intrigued. "Is it rude to ask what your other form is?"

Hēi Māo shook his head. "I'm a cat. My animal nature bleeds into my human nature." He grinned. "Which explains why I'm so good on the catwalk."

Nala laughed as he'd hoped she would.

"After years without any guidance for my other side, I was desperate to understand myself better," he explained. "So in June, I saw the opportunity to go out into the world and learn more about Jacque the cat."

"And how did that work for you?" Nala asked, leaning in. "Did you meet other shape-shifters?"

"I lived as a stray cat on the streets of Paris from mid-June until late September." He glanced at Brigitte, a secretive smile sneaking onto his face. "I didn't find any shape-shifters, at least none that I was aware of, so from that standpoint my adventure wasn't successful. But I met some really nice familiars and I found Brigitte." He was starting to feel good about the way the interview was going. They'd really only just started, but he was comfortable that they could do this.

"And how did you meet?" Madame Freis asked gesturing to the two of them. "Were you in your cat form?"

Hēi Māo looked at Brigitte. *You want to take this one?*

"At the beginning of the school year, I started looking for a familiar," his witch explained. "My magic has always wanted me to have a cat. And more importantly, it needed to be one who chose this path."

Nala's eyes went even wider than they had when he'd announced he was a shape-shifter. She couldn't seem to find the words she needed, but that was okay. His witch was on a roll.

"A delightful Birman familiar helped me meet all sorts of cats and kittens. It was kind of like a familiar dating service." Brigitte chuckled. She'd been so happy with his description of what it looked like, that she'd adopted it too. Pointing at him with her thumb, she continued. "He saw me, but hid."

"Miss Gigi saw right through me," Hēi Māo added. "She said I wasn't meant to be a stray, and she talked to me about what it meant to be a familiar." He shrugged. "What can I say, I was curious." He bumped his witch's shoulder with his. "And the more I watched Brigitte interact with other cats, the more I worried she would choose one of them." He looked down shyly, though he felt no such thing. He'd learned all about image from his father, and he needed them to see him as sweet and harmless. Not the monster so many shape-shifters were painted to be. "I'd watched her treat kittens for ear mites, feeding any of them who came near. She didn't just scoop up the first good candidate, and her respect for these possible life partners drew me in." He beamed at his witch. She was so good.

"This is all very sweet, but..." Nala straightened up, a move that took her posture from casual to attentive. One hand came up to lightly touch the earpiece that was surely ablaze with questions from the producer. "Are you telling us that you've become Brigitte's familiar?" Her words were carefully spaced, leaving no doubt of the meaning.

Hēi Māo grinned at her. "She brought me home, and with a little convincing, she agreed to bond with me."

"And did you tell her you were a shape-shifter?" Nala asked.

Brigitte raised her eyebrows at him. It really was only fair that he take this question every time it came up for the next fifty years or so.

He shook his head. "Having spent so little time freely in my cat form, I guess you could say I was a bit over-enthusiastic about it, and I'd impulsively decided to stay cat for the rest of my life." He sighed. "So this bit is on me. I didn't think it was important."

"He knows better now," Brigitte pointed out.

"Wow," Nala said, shaking her head a little. "I don't think any of us expected this as the reason for your absence."

Hēi Māo nodded. "Yeah. It's less dramatic than all the rumors that were going around."

"And you're **really** Brigitte's familiar?" Nala asked.

Hēi Māo nodded again.

"After several days with my family, he convinced me that he wanted to stay, and he wanted to be my familiar," Brigitte explained. "He doesn't go by Jacque anymore. We're actually in the process of legally changing his name to Tom Hēi, so that's what you'll see in his future shoots and appearances for Parenteau fashion."

"And who made that decision?" Nala asked, clearly aiming for the angle of an imbalanced dynamic.

"We made it together," Hēi Māo replied, glad Aalia had made them come up with an answer for that. "It's what I wanted. While I'm going to be modeling for my father part time again, I feel like the Jacque Parenteau stage of my life is over. Modeling isn't going to be my priority anymore, and changing my name reflects that."

* * *

There was a moment of silence before Nala found a line of questioning that worked for her, possibly from prompts through her earpiece. "Your time as witch and familiar has put you each in the spotlight, and it's only been about two months."

"Oh…" Brigitte said softly. "That's true." She suspected what was coming, and she hated it.

"We try not to focus on that too much," he added, using one of Aalia's recommended lines for redirecting the conversation.

"I believe we have footage of the first event," Nala said, looking to the screen on the wall. "It went viral, so everyone in Paris heard about you, Brigitte. And we all saw how you nearly lost your new familiar in an attack of cruel jealousy perpetrated by the mayor's daughter." The phone camera footage played, with most of the faces strategically blurred due to French privacy laws.

Hēi Māo wrapped an arm around Brigitte's shoulders when they watched him intercept Celeste's spell. She gasped, recoiling and turning away. *It's okay,* he whispered in her head. *I'm here. I'm safe. You saved me.*

"Are you okay, Brigitte?" Nala asked, sounding concerned, though Brigitte doubted the genuineness of the emotion. She definitely didn't have to show that clip, and she would need to look somewhere else the next time she needed a babysitter.

Brigitte nodded. "It's hard for me to watch that. It takes me back to the moment, and... it's awful." Her voice had gone rough, and she struggled to keep the tears from escaping.

"It's pretty awful for those of us who didn't directly experience it," Nala said.

"That was the first time I'd cast anything since bonding with Tom," Brigitte went on. "So it gave me a hint at how much he boosted my magic. I'd never been a low-power witch, but now..." She blew out a puff of air. "I'm revisiting all my old control exercises." Her smile was halfhearted, but it helped push the questions elsewhere.

"Sounds sensible," Nala agreed. "So, Tom, when did you tell Brigitte what you were?"

"Shortly after I rescued her from the Seine," Hēi Māo said. "It was kind of obvious at that point."

"Ah yes, the demon attack from late October. We have footage of that as well." Nala gestured to the screen again. "Please be advised that this may be disturbing to some viewers."

They'd seen it before, of course. She and Hēi Māo had both watched it a couple of times, mostly to prepare themselves should it show up somewhere unexpected. Though they were physically removed from the moment, watching as Brigitte's capelet fluttered in the arcane breeze, and she suddenly felt cold. He couldn't hold back the terror of losing her, and it flooded their bond, once again showing her exactly what drove him to do whatever it took to save her. Brigitte grasped his hand just before he let out a whine of distress. He buried his face in her neck, unable to watch himself fishing her out of the river and performing CPR on her. Frankly, she'd be fine if neither of them ever had to watch that scene again. It would always be too much.

"Is he okay?" Madame Freis asked quietly.

Brigitte's hand slipped into his hair. "He will be. It's just really upsetting for him, like watching the other clip was for me."

I came too close to losing you, he said.

I know how that feels. "So that's when I found out who and what he was, and Paris learned that Jacque Parenteau was still here," Brigitte said. "When I got out of the hospital, we sat down with my parents and some other folks, including Pierre Parenteau, to figure out what needed to happen before we went public with all of this. Pierre released a short statement letting Paris know his son was fine and would be returning to modeling, but he's going to be releasing another more significant message any minute. He kindly waited to let us share our story first." It had nothing to do with kindness and everything to do with strategy, but it was the lie they'd agreed to.

Hēi Māo straightened up then, still shaken but trying to move on.

"We have a few questions coming in from viewers," Nala said. "So let's find out what Paris wants to know." The screen went light blue, with black text popping up on it for all of them to read. "Ah yes. When you went missing, Tom, you had all of Paris looking for you. Fans, emergency services, private detectives. What do you have to say to them?"

"Oh." His eyes went wide, and Brigitte knew he hadn't even thought about that.

Apologize and deflect, she suggested.

"I'm really sorry." The uncertainty in his voice could probably be perceived as shame by those who didn't know him. "It was pretty selfish of me, and I hope you'll forgive me for being young and making rash decisions."

"Brigitte, this one's for you," Nala said as the screen changed. "What's it like to hang around with a supermodel all the time?"

Brigitte had to force herself not to roll her eyes at the inane question. She looked at him and shrugged. "It's just like hanging around my friends, I guess. I mean… we don't spend all our time doing each others' hair and makeup, so I tend to forget he's famous most of the time."

"We should totally do each others' hair," he suggested.

"Ooh," Nala said, rubbing her hands together after the screen changed again. "So are you two an item, then?"

"Urk," Brigitte gasped, which lead to coughing and she wrapped her arms around her ribs to support them. Aalia had warned them this could come up, but she'd blown it off as utterly vapid. "Up until two weeks ago, I thought he was just a really smart cat. And I think we'd have to be really cautious about something like that. It's not like we can break up and move on from each other."

Nala nodded. "That **would** be awkward. But I think Paris is rooting for the two of you." She resettled herself, turning away from the screen as it faded to white. "Now Tom, I've heard your father can be very difficult to work with, but that he's brilliant enough people are willing to do it anyway."

Brigitte didn't like that she'd brought his father into the discussion.

"He has very high expectations," he allowed.

"There are reasons why Parenteau is one of the top fashion houses in Paris," Brigitte added, pasting on a smile that felt too wide.

"And did your father's expectations of you have any role in your unannounced journey of self exploration?" Nala prodded.

"No?" he said quickly. "I mean, the big push was that I wanted to understand myself better, and he obviously couldn't help with that, so… that was his only involvement in me leaving."

Nala nodded. "You two have already had **quite** the adventure."

"We have," Brigitte agreed. "It's nice we don't have to deal with any big tabloid-worthy drama on top of that." She hoped her maman's friend got the message and drew back on her digging.

"And we kind of glossed over this earlier, but you, Brigitte, are our Mademoiselle Butterfly!" Nala said enthusiastically. "Everyone's been trying to identify that amazing young woman for weeks."

Brigitte let out a nervous laugh. "Yeah. That's me, all right."

"You were very brave," Nala said, nodding. "There's no telling how much damage that demon would have done if you hadn't stopped it. I've never heard of a sixteen year old witch banishing even lower level demons alone."

"Oh, I wasn't alone, though." Brigitte turned and smiled at Hēi Māo.

"It was your skill that focused it though," he pointed out.

"Why did you two choose to come forward with your story now?" Nala asked, clearly moving toward a wrap up to Brigitte's intense relief.

"We couldn't do it earlier, because Brigitte had to heal. And we needed to make some decisions about what we wanted to do going forward," Hēi Māo explained.

"Neither of us want to live a lie," Brigitte said. "Tom's going to start school with me, and honestly, people were probably going to figure it out. We wanted it to come out on our terms."

Nala nodded.

"And if it was going to come to light, I wanted to be sure **all** of it came out," Brigitte went on. This part she'd practiced heavily, because it was the most important message she could think of using her screen time for. "There's a lot of bias against shape-shifters. We all know they're disproportionately targeted by violent crime, and perpetrators get off with ridiculously light sentences. Tom is going to continue to be in the public view, and I wanted to be sure people associate him with Mademoiselle Butterfly. I will not hesitate to protect him, or any other shape-shifter who needs it."

Chapter Thirty-Two

"You really don't have to do this," Brigitte insisted.

Her father hugged her from the side. "Of **course** I do."

"We're perfectly capable of walking a few short blocks without something going wrong," she said. "I mean, we've been taking regular walks and haven't gotten attacked by anything in **weeks**."

"That's not why I'm here," he said, ushering her and Hēi Māo across the street the moment the light changed.

"You already registered him," she pointed out.

"I did," he confirmed, smiling happily.

"And the media know we're off-limits," she said, relieved that Madame Chien reviewed French privacy law with her. She glanced at Hēi Māo as he wrapped her hand in his. She wasn't sure if he'd noticed, but some of the kids standing around outside the building were starting to stare.

"Yes. And detective DuValle has asked that we immediately report violations on that front," her father said firmly. "Up by the sign if you please."

"Oh." It suddenly made sense. It was Hēi Māo's first day of school. Her parents were huge on photos of milestones, and they'd started a scrapbook just for him.

What are we doing? Hēi Māo wanted to know.

"Papa wants a photo for your scrapbook." She put her hands on his shoulders to move him into position. "There." She stepped back.

"Perfect," Paya said, snapping a photo with a digital camera that was nearly lost in his huge hand. "Now you go next to him, Cupcake. It's a big day for you, too." When he was finished he waved and promised to see them at lunch.

"Hey, Gitte, Hēi Māo!" Ruhul jogged up the sidewalk, Juniper bounding beside him. "Glad you could make it, and in dude form, too." He held out a fist to Hēi Māo.

Hēi Māo smiled and fist-bumped his new friend.

"Not that I mind you being a cat, when you want to be, but this," Ruhul gestured to the tall blond boy. "This means you've made progress with the things you needed to do. And Gitte's finally well enough to come to school. Also awesome." He leaned down so Juniper could climb his arm to her perch.

"Thank you for all your help, Ruhul," Brigitte gave him a quick hug.

"I'm always happy to help my best friends." He let go of Brigitte and looked at Hēi Māo. "That includes you, cat-dude. You need anything and Gitte's not able to help, I'm your guy."

Hēi Māo's cheeks turned pink, and he smiled, something more beautiful than what showed up in his professional model pictures. "Thanks, Ruhul."

"Anyway, as you may have noticed when you were last in the classroom, there's an empty seat right next to me in class," Ruhul pointed out. "It's got your name on it."

"I'd like that," Hēi Māo said. He looked at Brigitte. "Is it okay?"

She nodded before he could finish his sentence. "You don't have to ask me."

He blinked at her for a moment, then smiled. "Oh, yeah. Still getting used to that." He shrugged. "Years of being yelled at have kind of trained me wrong."

Ruhul scowled. "Not cool."

Brigitte reached up and ran her fingers into his hair just above his ear.

Ruhul pulled out his cell phone. "Oh, hey. Aalia's inside. Let's not keep her waiting."

More kids turned to gawk as they walked through the halls, and Hēi Māo took her hand again. *You okay?*

Just nervous, she sent back. *I want this to go well. I want people to see how wonderful you are and accept you for who you are.*

But you think they won't? he asked.

She shrugged. "Some will, some won't."

Ruhul glanced at her. "Talking behind my back?" he teased. He'd thought it was hilarious that Brigitte had trouble keeping her conversations with Hēi Māo either in her head or out where everyone could hear them.

She felt her cheeks go pink. "Sorry. Just freaking out a little, is all."

"No need to worry," Ruhul assured her. "Al and I have your back, and seriously, now that we all know you're Mademoiselle Butterfly, I don't think anyone's going to want to risk pissing you off by being rude to your familiar."

* * *

Madame LaMarr was standing behind the desk when they arrived. "Good morning," she said. "Are you Tom?"

Hēi Māo nodded. "Yes. That's me."

"It's a pleasure to have you in our class, Tom." He was surprised by how genuine she sounded.

184

"He's gonna sit with me, ma'am," Ruhul said. "I'm going to show him the ropes and all that."

"Thank you, Ruhul." She nodded to him. "I know we can count on you." She turned her eyes back to Hēi Māo. "We're going to have you take some assessment tests in these first few days so we know where you're at academically."

Brigitte snickered. "He's been helping me with my studies, ma'am. He's definitely **not** behind."

"Well depending on his results, I may need to give him more challenging material, then," Madame LaMarr said cheerfully. "And it's so good to have you back, Brigitte. Your absence has been felt."

"Thank you, ma'am." Brigitte nodded.

"You have permission to go to the nurse's office if you find yourself at all fatigued or overwhelmed." The teacher tilted her head. "I expect you to pay attention to your body's signals."

Hēi Māo liked her even more than he had before, and she'd been his favorite teacher when he'd visited Brigitte's classes as a cat.

"I don't think it'll be a problem," Brigitte said. "But I'll be careful."

I'm keeping my eye on you, Hēi Māo said. *Papa's right about you having trouble with that.* He grinned when she rolled her eyes in response.

The rest of the class filtered in after they took their seats, and most of the students stopped by the front row table to meet him.

"So you're a human and a cat?" Alexa asked, sounding excited. "That's totally wicked."

"Alexa! You can't just **say** things like that," a red-haired boy chastised.

Hēi Māo laughed. "It's okay," he insisted. "I don't mind questions if you're honestly curious."

"Yeah, but there's tact, and then there's Alexa." The boy

shook his head. "I'm Coren."

"Thanks for watching out for me, Coren," Hēi Māo said. "And yes, Alexa, I'm both a human **and** a cat."

"And you're still Brigitte's familiar when you're a human?" Alexa asked.

Hēi Māo nodded. "If you have magic, you should be able to see my bond." He brushed two fingers against his neck.

"Oh wow," Alexa said, squinting. "I wouldn't have noticed it if you hadn't pointed it out. But now that I see it, it's obvious."

The bell rang, starting Hēi Māo's first day of school, and the students hurried to their desks.

* * *

"Are you guys coming over for lunch?" Brigitte asked as she gathered up her things.

"Wouldn't miss it," Aalia promised.

"Excuse me, Brigitte?" Lucie had quietly come to stand by Hēi Māo's desk. She'd been Celeste's best, or possibly only, friend for years. Since Celeste hadn't been back, she'd been gradually opening up to other classmates a little at a time.

"Um... yes?"

"I wanted to thank you for what you did for Celeste," she said meekly. "She's never been very nice to you, and you could have responded so much harsher." She fiddled with a pale yellow envelope. "Thanks to you, she's finally getting the help she needs to be the person I know she can be, before it's too late."

Brigitte nodded, not really sure how to respond.

Lucie looked at Hēi Māo. "She's sorry about what she did to you, Tom. She said it was a wake-up call, especially now that she knows who you are. And now that she knows what Brigitte could have done to her, she's... grateful for your restraint." She held out the envelope to Brigitte. "She asked me to get this to you."

Brigitte stared down at the envelope, slowly reaching for it. "You've been visiting her?"

Lucie nodded. "Every other day. She's already come so far, but she'll be... um... out for the rest of the school year, and probably the start of next year."

The paper bore no hint of magic, so Brigitte took it. "You're a good friend, Lucie."

Lucie finally smiled, looking relieved. "I'll see you all after lunch." She waved and turned to head out.

Brigitte waited until after she'd eaten to open the envelope. It was a flowery letter of apology. It was strange to be able to tell this was from her long-time bully, because the language was so very Celeste, but it was also gracious and grateful without a single snide or backhanded remark.

Chapter Thirty-Three

On the way to their last class of the day, Brigitte stopped into the bathroom, leaving Hēi Māo waiting in the hallway. When she came out, she found a ring of students around him and a boy from the next grade up. That was never a good sign. She didn't know the guy's name, but she'd seen him around. He reminded her of one of those awful American tourists, flaunting his wealth and loudly sharing his opinions with anyone in the vicinity, whether they wanted them or not. Right now, he was toe-to-toe with Hēi Māo, an ugly sneer on his face.

To his credit, Hēi Māo seemed relatively unconcerned by whatever this was. She caught a trace on tension from him, but nothing else.

"**You** don't belong here," the boy said. "My family will spare no expense to get you and that witch of yours thrown out."

"Good luck with that," Hēi Māo said calmly. "I'm pretty sure most of Paris will turn on your family like rabid hyenas if you go after Mademoiselle Butterfly. She's **very** well liked."

The jerk scowled and stepped closer. "**She** may be, but **you** aren't."

"I have at least three different fan clubs," Hēi Māo pointed out. "How many do you have?"

That was met with a low, "Ooooooh," from the gathered crowd.

Furious, Brigitte started pushing her way into the circle of students. "Excuse me. I need to get through."

"If you keep showing up at L'Étoile du Nord, one of you is going to get hurt," the jerk snarled, jabbing Hēi Māo in the center of his chest. "You wouldn't want your witch's face getting scarred up, would you. Or yours, for that matter."

Hēi Māo's hand shot out and grabbed the front of the guy's shirt. Then he spun and slammed the other student against the wall, his feet a few inches off the floor. "**You** do not get to threaten her." His voice was colder than she'd ever heard it. "You seem to have mistaken me for some tame house cat, but I won't spook at your posturing." He dropped the guy. "Stay away from me, and don't come snuffling around my witch." He flicked his hand open in front of the jerk's face, and black sparkles of power flickered around his fingertips. Though she'd heard about his ability to curse things with misfortune, she'd never seen it before. Closing his hand, the magic vanished. He looked up and saw her at the edge of the crowd. "Ready for class?" he asked as if nothing had just happened.

She stared at him in surprise for a moment. *What was that?*

I'm your familiar, he pointed out. *It's my job to protect you.* He looped his arm through hers and started down the hall with her.

"And it's mine to protect you," she reminded him. *How are you so calm about this?*

Madame Wheeler and I talked about how to deal with people like him, he explained.

She was really glad his therapist had thought about that.

"After working with my father and his associates for years, and facing off with that demon, guys like that aren't all that

189

frightening." He shrugged.

"I can see that." Her own scale of scary things had been irreparably skewed in the last two months.

"Besides, that guy's going to have an awful day," Hēi Māo said cheerfully.

She grinned. "Yeah. I'm going to report him to administration during class." Considering how the school had handled Celeste for years, Brigitte expected anti-shifter issues to be brushed off. Since her history teacher, Monsieur Levale had proven himself a champion for shape-shifters, she'd e-mailed him for suggestions while she was still convalescing. His helpful advice had resulted in a letter from Madame Chien reminding the administration of the legal considerations of Hēi Māo's status. She raised the threat of lodging a complaint with the Ministry of National Education should the school fail in its duty to protect minority and marginalized students. The response from the deputy headmistress was very reassuring.

"Oh, that's good idea," Hēi Māo said with a nod.

"Wait, isn't that what you were talking about?" she asked.

He beamed at her. "He's had a run in with bad luck." He shrugged. "He should be more careful about touching black cats in the future. It can be **so** hard to control."

Chapter Thirty-Four

Brigitte carefully pinned Hēi Māo's white pin-striped pants to allow a full break. Friedric, the primary tailor for the Parenteau brand, stood behind her, ready to offer recommendations as he had with the last few fittings. For now, he was silent. Once the Parenteau staff were informed that Hēi Māo was bound as a familiar, those with magic excused themselves from touching him. It was a rule they were unwilling to bend on. The non-magic staff quickly followed suit given the cultural sensitivity of the issue, or so they claimed. Brigitte suspected it was just a sneaky way to defy their boss. Either way, it resulted in Brigitte helping with the pinning and touching part of any tailoring of Parenteau items Hēi Māo wore.

"That's deftly done, Miss Brigitte," Friedric said when she stood up and gestured for Hēi Māo to turn around.

"Thank you." Until she was sure the hem was right, she didn't look away. "It's a relief to know I've been doing it right."

"That you have." He nodded to Hēi Māo. "Go ahead and doff those, my lad. I'll get them finished while you get on with whatever else you need to do."

As she'd gotten quite used to him doing at photo shoots and

other modeling activities, he stripped then and there, handing the clothes to Brigitte to pass to the tailor.

" Mademoiselle Defresne-Li?" Monsieur Parenteau's voice wasn't raised, but she could hear it as if it were. Whether she liked it or not, he did have a commanding presence. She looked up to see him crossing the room. "I wish to see how your final design has turned out before I clear it for the catwalk."

It was a formality, one they'd been through once already. "Do you want to go get it, Kitty?" she asked, touching his bare shoulder. She'd gotten used to comforting and shielding him from his father. She also loved the sour look on Monsieur Parenteau's face when she called Hēi Māo, Kitty. She turned back to find him closely watching Hēi Māo, his eyes narrowed slightly. "Is there something wrong?" she asked.

Monsieur Parenteau redirected his attention down at her. "He's had a growth spurt."

Brigitte nodded. "He's nearly seventeen. That happens. I sent Friedric his new measurements last week."

Hēi Māo brought over the garment bag, clearly avoiding his father's eyes.

Laying the bag on her workspace, Brigitte swiftly opened it, trying to get this over with as quickly as she could.

"What do you weigh in at these days, Jacque?" Monsieur Parenteau asked.

"Don't be rude, Monsieur Parenteau," Brigitte said quietly, careful to keep her voice below the general noise of the room. She detested the man, but she didn't feel there was any benefit to antagonizing him on purpose, though he clearly had no such concerns. "You know he's not using that name."

"I apologize," he said smoothly. It had become routine. He would misname Hēi Māo intentionally. She would call him out, to the surprise of his staff, and he'd throw a completely insincere apology at them. "Tom, then. What's your current weight."

Hēi Māo shrugged. "I've no idea."

"He's been growing up, sir, not out," Brigitte said, rolling her eyes. "As you can see, he's all lean muscle." She waved at his body. *Go ahead and put it on. The sooner he sees it, the sooner we can go.*

Hēi Māo had the black leather pants on and was about to pull on a lime green v-neck shirt, when Monsieur Parenteau reached forward, but didn't touch his son. "Stop a moment," he said, his voice clinical and emotionless. "Mind your posture, please." Hēi Māo straightened up. Monsieur Parenteau tapped one finger against his lips. "You are thriving, aren't you." It wasn't a question. "At this rate, you'll be able to start picking up adult swimwear and topless jobs in three months, easily."

"We'll talk about it and get back to you on it," Brigitte said, feeling that Hēi Māo had gone into a flurry of confusion over what was probably the closest he'd gotten to praise from his father ever.

Monsieur Parenteau nodded to Brigitte. "I'll e-mail you the contract so you have the full information. It will involve a substantial bump in pay."

Brigitte nodded. "We'd appreciate that information." As long as Hēi Māo wanted to model, she'd let him, but it would be on his terms. Though in his father's case, she was happy to make it appear as though they were her terms. *Finish up, Kitty.*

Hēi Māo pulled on the shirt, and the soft fabric clung to his frame perfectly. She loved this material for that very reason. Finally, he pulled on the jacket, trim fitting black leather that she had pieced together so the seams added to the design.

"Short walk, please," Monsieur Parenteau said.

Hēi Māo walked across the room, his feline grace fluid and smooth. He performed his perfect turns, holding the jacket open, then sweeping it off to toss over his shoulder for the walk back.

"Very good, Mademoiselle Defresne-Li," Monsieur Parenteau said. "We will see both of you here tomorrow evening at six."

Brigitte nodded, livid that he could so easily compliment her without ever mentioning Hēi Māo's contribution. She'd half-expected Monsieur Parenteau to reject the completed leather outfit, just to test Hēi Māo's limits, but perhaps he realized that would lose him a talented model for the show. She returned the outfit to its hangers, taking great care in ensuring the folds and drapes were all in the right places. *Is it wrong that I keep expecting him to sabotage me?* she asked as she tucked the clothes into the garment bag.

Sounds reasonable to me, he replied. *I don't think it would be the first time.*

She'd been suspicious, but didn't have a reason to worry until he mentioned that. *Should we have a backup plan?*

I have one.

She glanced over to where he was pulling on his shoes. *You do?*

I can make anything look good. He wasn't wrong there. It had turned out that her familiar was a supermodel both because of his looks and because of his skill. *And your work is brilliant. If we arrive the morning of a show and your pieces are damaged, you'll turn them into something new or I'll wear them as is, and we'll call it art.*

Amused, but strangely reassured by his off-the-cuff plan, she zipped up the garment bag and went to return it to the rack with the other show pieces. *I think I'll bring one of the rejected pieces tomorrow as a spare.*

Brilliant. Now we have two backup plans.

By the time she was done putting the outfit away, Hēi Māo was waiting for her. He took her hand to lead her out of the building while she silently stewed.

"How long do you want to model for Pierre?" she asked, as they headed for the train station.

194

He shrugged. "I guess, until you get enough exposure that you don't need him anymore." He smiled proudly. "Then I'd like to mostly work for Butterfly."

She liked the idea of him continuing to work on her line. "You don't have to model for me," she said. They'd talked about it before, but she wanted to reiterate her point. "You're really good at it, and I appreciate it so much. But I want you doing something you enjoy."

He reached out and booped her nose with one finger. "I like modeling when I have a choice about it, but it's a limited term field. The way the industry runs, I've only got ten, maybe fifteen years left, if I'm lucky. I may as well take advantage while I'm in favor, and it'll build our savings. I've been thinking of studying business for later. I like the math and the demographic studies parts."

He'd been brilliant with math, though to be fair, she had yet to see a subject he floundered in. "Business, huh?"

He nodded. "Yeah. That way you can just focus on the design side of Butterfly, and I can take care of the business side." He beamed at her, clearly proud of his plan. "We're a team."

* * *

Hēi Māo sat in his place at the desk he shared with Brigitte, happily working through the day's homework. He'd helped her reorganize their room during her recovery to make sure they both had their own space, though they were often content to overlap. The area under the loft had become his, much of it taken up by his twin bed. His dresser displaced her sewing nook, but they'd kept the longer section of desk, dividing it between them. It was much simpler than the obnoxiously huge desk he'd had in his father's house, and it suited him. He felt a little bad about needing to set up a replacement space for her sewing machine, a new wall-mounted desk on the other side of his cat castle, but she'd been very clear that she was happy with it. She was planning to make a set of curtains to enclose his area when he wanted privacy, and he was excited about picking out the fabric in the next few days.

"Hey, Kitty?" Brigitte said, catching his attention. She frowned at her tablet, chewing on her thumb. "Did you understand today's physics lesson?"

"Oh, yeah." He pushed his chair closer to her. "Need an alternate explanation?"

She nodded. "I thought I understood, but..." She shook her head. "Now that I'm doing the homework, it's pretty clear I missed something critical."

"Let's review from the textbook first," he suggested. "It's more important that you understand the concepts than just the math."

"You're really smart, you know that?" she asked, tapping at her tablet to pull up the digital textbook.

"Could we start my magic lessons soon?" he asked. She'd left it up to him, and he was ready to learn. Magic with her was wonderful, and if Master Fu was right, and he had untapped magical skills, he wanted to discover them.

"When we wrap up our homework, we'll start the basics of your arcane teachings," she promised. "Just let me know if I go too fast or overload you." She patted his back. "It should be something you get to enjoy."

"Yes!" He bounced in his chair. "Best academic day, ever."

She giggled. "You're a very silly kitty sometimes."

"Silly kitties are the best kitties," he assured her, flopping over her lap as though he were a cat instead of a boy. He rolled over so he was draped on her in some sort of warped back bend. "Trust me. I know what I'm talking about."